Pivotal Paths

Laurence Perry

PIVOTAL PATHS

ISBN : 978-0-9991454-0-1

Printed in the United States of America 2017

Contents

Acknowledgement

To the lovely ladies who grace my existence. My mother Robbie Perry the Queen who gave me life, provided me with the example responsible for the strength, determined work ethic, and capacity to love I proudly possess. My big sister Sharon who continuously provides a guiding hand from her esteemed seat by the creator's side. Love you sis. LaRohnda and Misty, time, distance, and the devil try as they may are no match for we remain bonded by the ropes of love woven thick by the Matriarch of our family. Love your lives more than I love my own. To my tender experience who equipped with nothing more than a rain coat and tender soul stepped into the grey skied storm that shadowed my existence and courageously braved its elements. I extend unfettered appreciations. You are truly invaluable.

My brothers Derek and Bryant not many words are spoken for we are man of much machismo. Not a problem, though implied it is not necessary the love runs deep. For I guided by the hands of a proud tradition am indeed my brothers keepers. My adopted brothers, those who stalked the concretes of madness by my side for years on top of years. Those who broke the mode with progressive defiance. Edward Akili Gammage as you stated in your courageously incubated catabu, we are connected till death. Your profound words express my own sentiments and I quote, "you are friend rarely found in prison. A friend whom I owe much for being that person who understood direction, purpose, and the importance of positive dialogue." Brother we pushed one another in ways that helped us maintain determined focus to transcend the insanity that permeated our circumstances. The struggle continues.

Anthony Anu Ra Robinson my brother your calming presence and loyal nature fronted me like a closet mirror. You were that good conscience that consistently counseled me off the edge of darkness that so often confines us ghetto dwellers to counter productivity. Your commitment and example (I watched as you evolved from a good to a great poet) provided great inspiration. Then there was Rip.

My young rap star, you were there from this projects inception till its completion. You heard stories and witnessed moments of elation and frustration. I bounced ideas off of you and reached productive conclusions as a result. Thank you brother. Last, but definitely not least my son, nephew's, and niece's this book is for you all in hopes that its realistic examples serve as enlightenment. Love you all.

PROLOGUE

Quic leaned against the dented trunk of a broken-down Buick underneath the carport in the rear of the Wilmington Arms apartment complex, waiting for his homeboy Red. It was five after five in the evening, and he was minutes away from losing his virginity. "Boyz n the Hood" played across the screen of his mind's eye. Trey was in the backseat of Doh Boy's low rider preparing to do his part in avenging Ricky's death – hood life, hood strife.

"Quic," a high-pitched voice brought him back to the moment. "What's up with you, Cuz? Where da fuck you at?"

"Huh? Wha, what's up, homie?" Quic looked a little puzzled.

"Where you at, Cuz?" Red said laughing. He knew that Quic was a ball of nerves.

"Nowhere, I'm just posted."

Red pulled his Raiders cap low on his forehead and took a seat next to Quic. "You got the address?"

Quic nodded as he fished into his pants pocket and gave Red a folded piece of paper.

Red grabbed the paper and looked at Quic through intense hazel eyes. "You think we can catch that fool at this time?"

"He should be on deck. Basketball season is over."

"We will see." Red lowered his head and studied the address.

Quic adjusted the black beanie he was wearing and then folded his arms across his chest. He could not sit still. He was ready to get the shit over with. "Red," he called. "What we waiting on?"

"Be patient, homie. The fool ain't going nowhere. We gonna get that ass." Red chuckled. "Nah, Cuz. We waitin' on T-loc. Cuz went to get the ride. He'll see back in a minute."

"Okay." Quic looked down at his black Nike Cortezes.

Quic and Red both were geared in all black and looked like television cat burglars. Both sported Dickies and Cortezes. Quic wore a T-shirt while Red wore a sweatshirt. It wasn't cold out, but Red wanted to hide as much of his near white skin as he possibly could.

T-loc swooped up in his mom's four-door Nissan Maxima bumping N.W.A.'s "Straight Outta Compton" and called out, "Yaah, what up, Cuz?"

"Yaah!" Red called back.

Quic didn't say anything. He just nodded while taking to his feet and walking towards the car. He got in the back while Red took to the passenger's seat.

"What's up, Tim?" Quic said once he was seated.

"This square ass nigga call a nigga by his real name and shit," T-loc said laughing. "What's hattenin' though, ma nigga?" T-loc reached his clenched fist over the seat and gave Quic a pound.

"Shit." Quic kept it simple. He didn't like being clowned but chose to let it slide for the sake of the mission.

Red pulled two guns from his waist and looked to T-loc. "You got yo shit?"

T-loc answered by lifting his shirt and revealing the pearl handle of a nickel-plated .45.

"Yaah, that's right, homie." Red took one of the guns he'd pulled from his waist and handed it over the seat to Quic.

The gun was a blue steel 44 magnum. Quic took hold of it and stared in genuine amazement. The gun looked like something off a Clint Eastwood movie.

T-loc turned the car around, and the trio was on its way. In less than five minutes, they were in Cedar block pushing up Brazil reading addresses.

"Turn that shit down homie. We don't wanna spook these niggas." Red said referring to the N.W.A. that T-loc was still bumping.

T-loc complied, but he wasn't worried. The Maxima's deep burgundy paint was the perfect camouflage for the young Crips stalking Piru territory.

Quic and the fellas were not on the typical blue hunting red mission. They were on the hunt for a particular Piru. His name was Motoroil, and he'd committed the ultimate sin of ratting on Lil Jay. Lil Jay was now in Los Padrinos Juvenile Hall facing a life sentence and desperately needed Motoroil to disappear.

Red was studying addresses while Quic continued to stare at the 44 that rested in his lap when T-loc demanded their attention. "Cuz, y'all see that?"

"What?" Red said continuing to read addresses through squinted eyes. "We like three houses away."

"Look, Cuz!"

Red looked up and ahead. "Damn!" He exclaimed.

Quic remained silent, but his eyes grew wide at the site of ten to 15 mean mugging brothers draped in variations of red, burgundy, and black shooting dice in a driveway a few houses ahead.

"Damn, Cuz," Red repeated looking at the paper he'd got from Quic. "That's Cuz house."

"What?" T-loc slowed his approach.

"Nah, Cuz, don't slow up." Red's words were rushed.

T-loc hit the gas and drove past the crowd. The Pirus didn't seem to be paying any attention. They were too engrossed in the dice game.

Red turned around to face Quic. "Was Cuz out there?" Quic was the only person in the car who knew who Motoroil was.

"Yeah, he was the one in the red hooded sweatshirt. The one who was on the dice."

T-loc kept driving till Brazil ran out giving way via left turn to Kemp Ave. He made the turn and pulled over to await further instructions.

"Look, Cuz, bust a U and drive back by. We will just light all of them mothafuckas up," Red said.

"Nah, Cuz. We can't buss out the car. This ma mom's shit. I can't do her like that." T-loc shook his head from side to side.

"Why the fuck did you drive your mom's shit in the first place?" Red's skin turned the color of his name.

"You needed a ride, and this shit had to happen today." Quic's mind drifted back to "Boyz n the Hood" while Red and T-loc argued.

Trey's eyes grew sad and fear crossed his expression. "Let me out," he said.

Doh Boy pulled to the curb and let Trey out. He and the other passengers continued the mission.

"Fuck it, Cuz. Come on, Quic. We gonna walk back around there and serve these niggas," Red said. "Stay here, Loc. Keep the car running and be ready in case these fools buss back."

The plan was set, and it was time to get crackin'.

Chapter One

Shining Star

Ten seconds showed on the digital timer. The Tarbabes were down by one to Perennial High School basketball powerhouse Dominguez Dons.

The Tarbabes worst free through shooter Derek Banks was at the free-throw line. The 6'6 center that shot free-throws at a clip more horrific than Shaquille O'Neal had an opportunity to help his team pull off the biggest upset of the young season.

Both teams were in the midst of streaks that going back to the previous season stretched into double digits in the opposite direction.

"Badunk," the frozen rope shot thudded against the front of the rim and crashed to the hardwood.

The crowd of twenty or so people sighed their collective disappointment. The second free-throw, another frozen rope, hit the back of the rim and swirled for two seconds before popping back out and into the hands of the Don's well positioned seven-foot center Darrell Jackson.

Darrell cradled the ball and waited for the foul. He was stunned when the ball suddenly flew from his grasp and bounced on the hardwood. The Tarbabe's star point guard called Quic for his often-unmatched speed had crept up punched the ball free and before Darrell knew what was happening picked it up and finger rolled it into the hoop.

The crowd leaped to their feet and began screaming at the top of their lungs. Their team was on the cusp of securing a long-awaited victory. The Don's coach slammed his clipboard and called a time-out. He collared Darrell and scolded him for not securing the ball. The Tarbabe's coach down at the other end of the court was just as animated. He grabbed his star player by the arm and said, "Good work, kid, but this ain't over. You gotta go out there and get one mo' steal." He lifted his clipboard and went on. "Their center is gonna inbound. He's a giant that towers our entire squad. We won't be able to impede his inbound. We, therefore, won't even trip off him. Derek will double any open player. They are gonna run several picks. Switch them all. Our D is good enough. Let's get this win."

The Don's advanced the ball and the play went exactly as the Tarbabe's coach had predicted. The Don's guards ran a pick and roll that gave the impression that one was open. Darrell made the pass, and as soon as the ball left his hands, he tried to pull it back. Quic having played possum jumped the lane and snagged the steal. The game was over, the Tarbabe's were the victor. They had impressively toppled the king of the hill.

The Tarbabe's had broken a 13-game losing streak with style. The small high school gymnasium erupted into pure pandemonium.

The audiences' members rushed the court to celebrate with their team.

●●●

"What ch'all wanna do, Cuz?" The Tarbabe's outspoken two guard, Lil Jay, asked his teammates as he tied the navy-blue shoe strings of his Chucks. He and the other members of the team had showered, dressed, and were ready for the after-game festivities.

"Whatever," Quic was the first to respond. The other team members expressed similar sentiments.

Lil Jay suggested Chico's pizza in Lynwood, while someone else recommended Skate land over on Piru Street. Lil Jay lit into him. "Cuz you know a nigga can't go to that mothafucka!" Lil Jay was an unabashed Crip. There was no way in hell he was going to the place that was known as Piru headquarters. Lil Jay was a rider, but he was not stupid.

The team entertained a couple of other potential destinations such as Skate Depot in Cerritos and Cal Bowl in Long Beach before settling on Chico's Pizza. Hunger pangs had proven the deciding factor.

There were two cars available to the guys; Dexter Thomas had his dad's Buick Skylark while Lil Jay had his own 1976 Impala. They were good though. Piling twelve into two cars would not be too difficult. They would just roll six to a car.

Quic grabbed shotgun in the Impala. There had been no need to call dibs as the spot was his. He and Lil Jay were best friends. They had been best friends since grade school when Quic had backed Lil Jay in a mini melee at Longfellow Elementary School.

Quic was the total opposite of Lil Jay in many ways. Where Jay was outgoing and aggressive Quic was quiet and reserved. Though both grew up in Park Village, Quic did not gang bang. Unlike Lil Jay, Quic had dedicated himself to sports. He dreamed of getting his mom and little brother out of the hood.

Lil Jay made the right turn off Long Beach Boulevard into Chico's narrowed mouthed parking lot. He drove slowly careful not to tear his straight laces on 520's up in any of the potholes that graced the unkempt grounds.

After finding a place to park Lil Jay instructed his teammates to go ahead and enter while he stayed behind to retrieve his 9mm master charge from it stash spot underneath the dashboard.

Inside of Chico's the Tarbabes grabbed four nearby tables. The tables were tiny, and though they had place mats for four, they looked big enough to only provide a comfortable fit for two. The fellas weren't tripping though; they would use their ghetto resourcefulness to go Ray Charles and make it do what it does.

Despite its small tables, Chico's interior was extremely roomy. There was a family side and an adult side. The walls of the family side were lined with video games and pinball machines while the adult side had pool tables, served beer, and required identification.

The team pooled its resources to buy several pizza pies and pitchers of soda. Lil Jay, a hood hustler, carried the bulk of the load. The others all were still pretty much dependent on their parents.

They all got super full and were competing against one another at Ms. Pacman when Chico's front door opened and gave way to the entrance of Tarbabe's arch rival and Lil Jay personal enemy, Motoroil. Motoroil was the star two guard for the Centennial Apaches, who had Piru ties.

"All, hell nah," Lil Jay hissed through tight lips.

His game went south. The red ghost trapped his Ms. Pacman in the corner and "beeruppp." He was out. Jay slapped the joystick hard enough to break it. He turned from the game and went to Motoroil. "What's hattenin', Cuz? You a little out of bounds, huh."

"What's up, man?" The kid whose complexion matched his name smiled showing all teeth.

Motoroil wasn't afraid of Lil Jay. He was out-numbered and out of bounds as Chico's was in Palm and Oak Crip territory. His approach was purely strategic.

"What choo doin' ova here?" Lil Jay pressed hoping to provoke Motoroil.

"Heard y'all knocked the D off." Motoroil ignored Jay's provocations.

Jay smiled. He couldn't help but respect Motoroil's tactical prowess. The other Tarbabe's cheered loudly. They too wanted to avoid the incident. Dexter, a Palmer block Crip, was the only other Tarbabe who gang banged. The others would participate if something popped though. They did not have a choice.

"Don't get too happy. Y'all still gotta be ah mean see the tin," Motoroil said.

Lil Jay caught the slip. He laughed and said, "Y'all just don't cee scared to show up."

"Ha, ha, we will be there and remember that y'all gotta come to the tin, too."

"The Hub city's real Crips ain't neva scared," Lil Jay shot back.

A vanilla cream-complexioned, exotically beautiful girl with green eyes walked up, put her arm around Motoroil's waist, looked across from her and said, "Hey Michael."

"What's up, Tasha?" Quic responded as all eyes turned in his direction.

Tasha was a friend of Quic's who lived in the Mob. The two had met a couple years back when both attended the Youth Action Center a program sponsored by the city of Compton designed to keep youth out of trouble.

Tasha was not only gorgeous in the face; she had a nice body as well. She stood 5'1" and weighed about 120. She was thick in all the right places. Quic smiled as he remembered the big crush he'd always had on Tasha. He'd never acted on it though; he'd been intimidated.

The exchange between Quic and Tasha broke the tension and allowed the respective parties to go about their business.

The Tarbabe's went on to enjoy the remainder of their evening. Their star shined bright and they assumed success was on the horizon.

Chapter Two

One Win

Compton High buzzed with excitement. Everyone from the faculty to the student body was intoxicated with school pride. Their basketball team had beaten the cities best and in the process personified the change that Sam Cook sang about.

Quic was the school's Michael Jordan. His game-winning heroics had earned him instant celebrity status. "Congratulations and Good games," were rained on him and his teammates like an unforgiving hailstorm.

Quic expressed sincere appreciation with a smile on his face, but he really didn't like all the attention. He was a person who embraced obscurity. He loved Jordan but would have preferred to have been Scottie Pippen.

"Damn, man! It's only one win," Quic stood on top of the cement bench taking stock of the school's preferred lunch area.

Lil Jay looked at Quic in surprise. "You crazy as fuck, Cuz. We beat the Dons. The fuckin' Dons, Cuz. Those fools were the shit. They hadn't lost a game in two years. We tapped dat ass. Cuz, we the shit. On PV." A light mist chased his words and hung in the air a second before disappearing into the grey-skied overcast.

Quic removed his hands from the pockets of his cowboy's starter jacket and pulled his navy-blue beanie lower on his head. "I know what you are saying Jay, but it's only one win. We ain't done nothing yet. We still got fourteen more games to play and let's not forget we already lost three."

"Damn negative Nelly. You can fuck up a wet dream." Lil Jay shook his head while smiling. His eyes were Asian tight as he was high as a kite.

"Hey y'all," a female voice interrupted Quic and Lil Jay from the rear.

Quic and Lil Jay turned to find Brenda West and her two friends Tracy and Cheryl. All three were Cripalets from Palmer block. All three were attractive girls that under different circumstances in a different community would have been top notch cheerleaders. Brenda, the hands down leader known for a vicious hand game that many dudes didn't even want to see was by far the most attractive. Her slightly flat oval face was home to a heart melting smile and big soft brown eyes. She had shoulder length hair that she never showcased choosing instead to sport braids. Her braids were always whipped and worked to enhance her attractiveness.

"What's crackin' with y'all?" Lil Jay responded.

"Y'all did y'all thing last night." Brenda folded her arms across her chest and shifted her weight to one foot causing her hip to poke out revealing a bubble-licious side view.

"Yea, we did." Lil Jay's smile widened.

Brenda laughed at Lil Jay's blatant arrogance. She then turned her eyes on Quic as if to say, *What's up with you?*

Quic shifted his weight from left to right then right back to the left. He pushed his hands back in his pockets and uttered a nearly inaudible, "Yep."

"Wait a minute. Y'all wasn't even at the game." Lil Jay took his boy's fade. He made sure that Brenda was looking at him before allowing his barely opened eyes to sweep her body.

Brenda's expression didn't change. She locked eyes with Lil Jay to get his attention. She then allowed her eyes to sweep over his body too.

"We heard about it."

"Man, y'all full of shit. Y'all only fuckin' wit us 'cause we won," Lil Jay said and laughed.

"Fuck you, nigga," Brenda said jokingly.

"Yea, nigga, you ain't do shit anyway. It was Quic who took them fools down." Tracy had spoken for the first time.

Quic wanted to laugh, but he couldn't do that to his boy. He just stayed quiet and continued to watch the show.

"You bitches wouldn't know if I did or didn't do anything 'cause y'all punk asses wasn't there. Real niggas can't get support from the home-girls. That's fucked up." Lil Jay cut his eyes at Tracy then back to Brenda.

"Whatever," Brenda waived Lil Jay off with a flick of her wrist before turning to walk away. Tracy and Cheryl spun on their heels and followed her.

"Damn, Cuz, that should be illegal," Lil Jay said and bit down on his lip.

"Man," Quic dragged the word out while shaking his head slowly in agreement.

"They should hold a hood ass contest. Them Palmer bitches would win first place," Lil Jay said with a laugh.

"Don't forget about the home girls and all the other sister's in the various hoods. Shit, ass is just a black thang period, but on the real though, Brenda, Tracy, and Cheryl got it good."

●●●

The congratulations and giddy school pride left Quic with a weighty mind. The team had won one game, a big one, but only one. He wanted the team to be the best like everyone else did. However, he was not lost on the fact that the team coming off a thirteen-game losing streak was only one and three on the season. The celebratory elation was warranted to a degree. The team still had fourteen games left. They had a lot more work to do. Cautious optimism would be more appropriate.

Quic expressed his concerns to coach White before practice. Coach White was in complete agreement. He decided that he would turn the pre-practice talk over to Quic so that Quic could share his sentiments with the team. They needed to hear them and coach thought that they would be better received from a peer.

Coach White gathered the squad up around the free throw line. "Quiet! Get quiet, guys." He paused while they settled down. "Quic is gonna do the pre-practice talk today. Give him your undivided attention."

Quic walked to the center of the circle. "Ummp um. Pa Peep game y'all. Look, on some real shit, fuck what anyone outside of this locker room is talking about. We beat Dominguez and, yes, that was a bomb ass win."

The team interrupted him with celebratory cheers and loud applause. Quic waived his arms to quiet them before continuing. "It doesn't mean shit if we don't keep this shit going. That's only one win in an eighteen-game season. Our record right now is bullshit - one and three. We are still under 500. Plus, we were up by a dove at half-time and let those fools come back and almost win. We got a lot of work to do. We should have won that game with ease. I don't know about y'all, but I got a taste of winning and I like that shit. We beat the champs. Now, I want us to be the champs."

The team roared their agreements. Applause broke out once again. Quic waived them quiet once more before continuing. "We need to work on our defense. We need to work on our attitude. We need to think like winners. We need to work like winners. We need to become winners. We are the mothafuckin' Tarbabes!" He paused for three seconds then shouted at the top of his lungs, "Who are we?"

"Compton," a lone voice answered.

"Nah, nah, nah. Hell, the fuck nah. We the motha fucken Tarbabes! Now I ask again. Who are we?"

"Tarbabes. "The lone voice was joined by a few more.

"Fuck that. Come on, man! Who are we?"

"Tarbabes!"

"Who?"

"Tarbabes!" The team roared. Quic had them.

The team had a good practice. The backup squad was as pumped up as the starters. They gave them a serious challenge in the mandatory scrimmage session. Pier Brown the Tarbabe's backup guard made seven three-pointers in a row. Lil Jay was a three-point specialist in his own right. He matched the kid nearly shot for shot. Still, the backups were ahead.

Quic played on court coach and lit into Lil Jay, "Play some fuckin' defense on this, fool." Spittle chased the words.

"What!" Lil Jay glared at Quic through murderous eyes.

"Play some damn defense."

"I am playing mothafuckin' defense, nigga!" Lil Jay got nose to nose with Quic.

Quic didn't back down. "He using you."

"You stick him then, mothafucka."

Coach White stepped in to separate the best friends. He embraced their competitiveness but didn't want them to go too far.

"Finish the game."

"We good." Quic smiled at Lil Jay. He stepped around the coach and hugged his boy. He then whispered in Jay's ear, "I got him."

Quic picked Pier up on the inbound. He channeled his inner Gary Payton and gloved the freshman. Quic's speed made it impossible for the backup squad to get Pier the ball. The back-ups did not make another basket. The starters blew them away.

The inspired Tarbabes ran off three straight wins avenging one of their three losses in the process. They were now above 500.

Their next game was against undefeated Centennial who also had upset the Dons. This would prove a real test. Quic prayed that his teammates were up to it. He liked winning.

Chapter Three

The Real Deal

Friday night light's in the Hub City, a basketball extravaganza. Compton High School vs. Centennial High School, the Tarbabe's vs. the Apaches, Quic and Lil Jay vs. Motoroil and Co., Blue vs. Red, Crip, Blood; it was on.

The Tarbabe's were ready. They knew that a win against Centennial would solidify their status as a serious contender.

Centennial started the game clicking on all cylinders. They had their inside-out game going, and Motoroil was on fire. Their on-point offense coupled with Compton's own sluggish offensive efforts led to an early 10-point lead.

Lil Jay put forth his best defensive effort, but it wasn't enough. Motoroil hit three back to back three pointers with a hand in his face. Lil Jay tried to crowd him, but the 6'1 Motoroil who had the handle and quickness of a point guard lowered his head and drove to the rim. When help came, Motoroil dished for the assist. If help failed to come, he got the bucket.

Motoroil was a big mouth known for getting into opponent's heads by taunting them mercilessly. He was on Lil Jay from the jump. "Y'all some over rated bums," he spat time and time again.

Lil Jay's mumbling response remained the same, "Busta ass mothafucka."

The Tarbabes were down by 12 at the end of the first half. They meandered lazily into the locker room sporting dejected frowns and bowed heads. No one said a word.

The locker room was depressingly quiet until Coach White slammed his clipboard to the ground and yelled, "What the fuck is wrong with y'all. Quic is playing his ass off. He got 11 assists and ten points. But he ain't got no help. Plus, our defense is playing like shit.

Lil Jay is handling his business, but the rest of you mothafuckas are leaving him for dead when it comes to help."

He paused to take a deep breath. He then continued ranting similar sentiments for an additional five minutes. He concluded with a challenge for his team to come back and win the game. Sweat dripped down the coach's George Jefferson balding afro. As the team headed back to the court, Coach White pulled Quic to the side. "Can you stop him?"

Quic had known that coach was going to do this. The competitor in him was up for the challenge, but the side of him that was Lil Jay's best friend was not eager at all. He had no desire to upstage him. Also, at a small 5' 7", he was extremely disadvantaged.

"I think I can." was all he said.

"You sound unsure. You wanna just do what we been doing and see where it leads us?"

Quic thought about his best friend. The move would surely embarrass him, especially if Quic were to shut Motoroil down. Quic was torn. He did not want to embarrass Jay, but he did want to win;

desperately so. Quic knew that a win against the undefeated Apaches would be significant. "Nah, coach, put me on him."

Coach White smiled his satisfaction. He then pulled Lil Jay to the side to tell him what was up. Lil Jay was disappointed as anticipated and angrily pled his case for Coach to leave him on Motoroil to no avail. Coach wasn't having it. Lil Jay tried another approach. "That fool is too tall for Quic. He will have an obvious reach advantage."

"Yea, but Quic will have the speed advantage. Plus, you have the same advantage over their point guard. This will free you up on the offensive end. That's where we need you most right now. Our offense ain't doing shit, and you are our best shooter."

Lil Jay was sold. He nodded his agreement as if he really had a choice.

The plan worked to perfection. Lil Jay hounded the Apaches 5'6" point-guard like he was a defensive specialist, LeBron James on Tony Parker. Lil Jay pushed, pulled, and grabbed. This threw the Apaches offensive flow off.

Quic shadowed Motoroil staying one step behind to deceive the Apaches point guard. It worked. Soon as Apaches point guard, A.J. Green, thought he found a window and tried a bounce pass to Motoroil. Quic, with his tongue sticking out like Michael Jordan and showcasing Iverson speed, jumped the lane and snagged the steal. The steal led to an easy two. The comeback was on.

Compton's defensive pressure led to several easy buckets that helped their offense, catch fire. Lil Jay was in the zone. Centennial's 12-point lead was reversed and turned into a Tarbabe route. Motoroil and his teammates were livid. They lost all sense of sportsmanship. Routine fouls turned into hard fouls.

Quic grabbed the rebound on a missed three with twenty seconds left in the game. He walked it up slowly intent on letting the clock run out. The Tarbabes were up by nineteen. The game was over, but no one told Motoroil this. Motoroil went for a steal causing Quic to pick up his dribble. Quic looked to Coach White with arched eyebrows. Coach rolled his eyes and lifted his arms palms up just above his waist. Quic tried to turn his attention back to Motoroil but never made it. Motoroil stuck both palms in Quic's chest and shoved him to the ground.

Quic rolled onto his stomach and with both his face and fist balled up burpeed back to his feet. Motoroil passed him coming up. Lil Jay had come from behind and caught Motoroil with a solid right.

Both benches cleared, but the Compton security force acted quickly. They sprung to action and shut both benches down. When the smoke cleared, Quic and Lil Jay were surprised to have Brenda West and Tracy standing at their sides. The girls had attended the game. Quic and Lil Jay smiled their pleasure.

Coach White pulled his two stars aside and with a murderous frown spoke through clenched teeth, "Off the record, you did what the fuck you were supposed to do." He then opened his mouth and roared, "What were you thinking? There's no room in sports for shit like this."

Lil Jay suppressed a smile. It was cool to have Coach White's approval, but the truth was he really didn't give a damn if coach approved or not. Gangbanger or not, Quic was his ace; he'd always have his back.

After hitting the showers, the team got together and went to Chico's Pizza for what was becoming their victory ritual. Brenda and Tracy joined them at Lil Jay's invitation.

At Chico's, Lil Jay channeled his inner Macaroni Tony and went at Brenda. It took a couple hours of aggressive pursuit before he could usher her past the crush she had on Quic, but once he did she was his. He wasn't worried about Quic. Quic hadn't given him any indications that he was interested in Brenda.

While Lil Jay charmed Brenda, Quic played good ear available shoulder to a surprisingly stressed out Tracy. Quic was shy, but not gay. He peeped what Lil Jay was doing and was good with it. Tracy wasn't a bad consolation prize. Indeed, the caramel complexion girl with deep brown eyes and shoulder length curly hair catered more to his taste than Brenda did.

Quic wanted to get at Tracy, but his shyness rendered his push confusingly deliberate. Tracy didn't think he was into her. She, therefore, took the opportunity to talk about a relationship that really wasn't a relationship that she was involved in with a 30-year-old gangbanger she refused to name.

Quic didn't mind being the good listener; however, he was pissed at himself for being too damned shy. After they dropped the girls off Quic continuously chastised himself.

"Yaah, what up, Cuz?" Lil Jay smiling from ear to ear snatched Quic from his thoughts as they were pulling away from the curb in front of Brenda's house.

"Shit, tired as hell." Quic's response was less than inspired.

What's up with you and Tracy? Did you get the digits?"

"Nah, did you?"

"Hell yeah!"

Quic had just asked the question on the strength. He'd known damned well that his boy had got the digits. Shit, he'd peeped Lil Jay get a tongue kiss from Brenda. He couldn't help but feel a little envious.

Lil Jay waited a few seconds for a response. When he didn't get one, he spoke again. "Yea, Cuz, that's me. I bagged that. She Lady Jay now."

"That's right. I saw you on her."

Jay pulled in the parking space in front of Quic's home. "Yea, Cuz, I'm gone call it a night. See ya in the am."

"Fo sho, homie" Quic walked away licking his wounds.

Chapter Four

Good Kid

Quic nursed thoughts of the previous night's trouncing of the Apaches while manning the register at McDonald's. The team was on a five-game winning streak that included wins against the two teams that were considered the city's best.

As Quic sat looking in space through glossed eyes, he finally allowed himself a moment to envision his Tarbabe's as state champs. Sure, the team had more work to do. However, Quic believed that they could do it.

"Excuse me, sir," a soft voice interrupt Quic's thoughts.

Quic returned to reality with a smile on his face. "Hey T, what's going on?"

"What girl were you thinking about?" Tasha put her hands on her hips and tilted her head displaying a teasing smile.

"Why you ask that?" Quic asked surprised to see Tasha alone on Compton's west side.

"A man smiling the way you were while vacationing inside his own head has to be thinking about a girl." Tasha laughed good naturedly.

"You'd be surprised. What brings you on this side of town? Where's your dude?"

Tasha's expression turned serious. "Forget that jerk. We just broke up. I don't want to talk about him. How are you?"

"Tired as hell. Between basketball, school, and this gig I be whupped."

"I can imagine. Stick with it though, Michael. You have an opportunity to do something with your life. Don't be like these other drugs dealing gang banging bums whose futures will consist of long prison sentences or early deaths."

Quic saw the seriousness in what Tasha was saying, but he also recognized the hypocrisy. "You talking that shit, girl, but all you date is drug dealers and gang bangers."

A smirk crossed Tasha's hurt expression. "You don't know what you are talking about. You met one boy I've dated. Remember I was in the youth action center too, asshole."

Tasha was wrong, but Quic did not correct her he looked off into the distance, "You are absolutely right, and I apologize. I was out of pocket for that. I hope this doesn't sound insensitive, but I'm glad you broke up with that idiot. You are too smart and pretty for him."

"What?" Tasha's eyebrows furrowed and moved upwards. Quic's comment had caught her by complete surprise. He'd never given her any indication that he thought she was pretty.

"Can ju guys come on?" a Spanish-accented voice cut in. An older Mexican man standing behind Tasha was eager to make his order.

"Excuse you!" Tasha spent on the work weary guy who sported an oil-stained navy-blue khaki suit.

"Sorry, sir," Quic spoke before the man could respond. Quic had not been working for a month yet. He had no desire to lose the job.

Quic looked at Tracy and, in the lowest whisper he could muster, said, "Are you trying to get me fired and push me into being a drug dealing gang banger?" He hit her with a disarming smile then continued in a much louder voice, "What can I get you, ma'am?"

"I can wait. Let the anxious man go first." Tasha stepped aside and gave way for the Mexican guy. She was being sarcastic, of course; however, she also was not in a rush to end the conversation she and Quic were having.

The Mexican guy stepped up and made his order. Quic filled the order and got him out the way. He then took his break and sat at a table with her.

Tasha and Quic enjoyed another fifteen minutes of conversation before going their separate ways. Tasha wrote her phone number down and made Quic promise to call. He agreed.

Quic worked another five hours before his shift was up. He got his first check just before he clocked out. It was a whopping $163. He may as well have been rich; he felt like a serious high-roller.

Quic walked to the bus stop in front of the Shell's on Central and Rosecrans. The bus stop, like the McDonald's only two lots over, was in Piru territory. Quic was not concerned though. He did not bang. He could go anywhere that he wanted.

Quic had gotten hooked up with the McDonald's job through Red's big brother Randal. Randal was like an uncle to Quic. He'd been happy to help when Quic informed him of his desire to help his single mom who struggled while working through the day and attending night classes at Compton College.

Quic had waited for all of five minutes before he decided to two-foot it. He pushed up Central towards Compton Blvd. When he was in front of Jack in the Box, a burgundy Oldsmobile Cutlass pulled beside him. "What up blood? What that Campanella Park like?"

Quic turned to face the passenger and responded an uninspired, "What's up man?"

"Fuck crab!" the big blue-black brother who looked to be a direct descendant of the motherland growled.

Quic looked away and kept walking without responding. He was not a Crip, so the disrespectful term did not bother him.

The Pirus were certain that Quic was a Crip. They'd dissed Crip to get a rise out of him. They tried to shame him into an admission. They were aware that Crip protocol called for retaliatory action. Otherwise, they would be branded a buster.

Quic thought about Lil Jay. He smiled to himself thinking about the aggressive response Jay would have made. Such was the twisted psychology of the growing gang banging culture that was Crips and Bloods.

"A Blood, you hear me?" The passenger leaned his upper body out the window. He looked like a pure comedy to Quic. The mother land native had a Bill Cosby nose that was covered with sweat and acne. His eyes were hidden in the shadows cast by the brim of the red Philadelphia Philly's baseball cap he wore.

When Quic remained quiet, the passenger continued, "You must be a busta."

"Nah, man, I ain't no busta. I just don't gang bang," Quic's ego spoke for him.

"Yea, I bet you don't. Ha ha. You just one of those scary ass crabs that will flip the scrip when you wit yo busta ass homeboys on some deep shit. I should buss on yo bitch ass." He produced a nickel plated nine.

Quic shook his head from side to side before taking off running. He ran diagonally across the Central Compton Blvd. intersection.

"Boom! Boom! Boom!" The nine screamed after him.

The driver did not give chase though. He allowed the passenger to do his thing from where they were. When he'd emptied the clip, the driver busted a U-turn and went back toward Rosecrans.

Though Quic wasn't shook, he ran all the way to Wilmington. Once he was there, he went inside of Nix check cashing and turned his check into cash. Getting shot at in Compton, unfortunately, was an ordinary occurrence. Compton was like Vietnam minus the tanks and agent orange.

Quic entered the iron rod gates of the Wilmington Arms behind the 1972 Pontiac that belonged to old man George, the hood's bootleg liquor man.

Quic swaged up the boulevard like a big dog smiling from ear to ear. He was Eddie Levert with fat pockets living for the weekend.

"What's crackin', Quic?" Red greeted his approach.

"Shit, just chillin'. What's up with you?" Quic extended his right hand.

The two shook hands while pulling each other into a single armed embrace. Red pulled away first. "Hold on homie." He said before turning to go to a red Ford Granada.

Red stuck his head in the passenger window and after exchanging a few words reached into his back pocket to get a prescription pill bottle. He emptied some of the small white rocks from the bottle into his hand and gave them to the passenger. The passenger, in turn, handed Red three crumpled bills. Red stuffed the bills in his pocket and went back to Quic. Quic and Red were the same age. The two grew up together attending the same schools, playing little league sports and everything. Red, like Lil Jay, had picked up the blue flag choosing the Park Village Crip path. He was different than Lil Jay in that he was more drug dealer than gang banger. Red was serious about his money.

Red was deeply inspired by what he, Quic, Lil Jay and all the other young homies witnessed growing up in the Wilmington Arms. The older homies sold PCP and made a good living from it. They had plenty of low-riders and stylish clothes, sipped on forty ounces, and hosted a myriad of beautiful women. Red had baller dreams like Quic had hoop dreams.

"Where you comin' from, Cuzin?" Red asked Quic.

"Work."

"Oh yea, that's right. Randal hooked you up."

"Yep."

"How you like that shit? You over there with all those slob niggas." Red laughed.

"Yea, that don't matter. I do me."

"I feel you. When you gone shake that bullshit and come get some real bread?"

Quic looked down at his Nike's. Red had just deflated his $163 big dog ego. Folks in the hood looked down on minimum wage fast food jobs. They were considered the lowest of the low, a couple steps from welfare.

This wasn't the first time that Red had approached Quic about getting into the drug game. Red tried to recruit Quic every opportunity he got. Red was one of the few homeboys who did not stay on Quic about staying in school and sports to pursue his hoop dreams.

Quic had considered dealing drugs on several occasions. It was hard not to. The money was plentiful, and the work seemed easy. You just had to exchange rocks for cash and run if the police came.

Quic hadn't been playing organized basketball for that long. He'd never attended basketball camps. He'd never participated in the ALU programs. No sponsors or benefactors were providing free sports apparel. His mother brought his single pair of Nike's that he and she both prayed would last for at least half of the school year. Quic's family was as poor as the low-income apartments they lived in indicated.

Red looked into Quic's glossed eyes. He could see that Quic's wheels were spinning. "Look, Cuz."

Quic raised his head to see that Red had produced an off-white boulder a few inches larger than half of a golf ball.

"This is a quarter piece. It goes for $125, but I'll give it to you for a c-note."

"How much can I make off it?"

"Like $300 if you cut it right."

Quic had never touched crack before. He had no idea how to cut or sell it. Hell, he didn't even know what he was supposed to cut it with. However, turning $100 of his pay check into $300 sounded good. He could make it a onetime thing just to get ahead. "One hundred dollars?" Quic said each word slowly.

"Yep," Red had him. He handed Quic the boulder intent on closing the deal. "Shoot me the hundred when you make it."

"Naw, I got you right now." Quic dug into his pocket for his immature bankroll. He peeled off five twenty dollar bills and handed them to Red. He was in. "That's right, Cuz. Let's go upstairs so I can show you how to chop it up."

Red took Quic to the second-floor apartment in building J. The apartment belonged to a lady named Gale who supported her crack habit by opening her house to the dealers. Gale's apartment was an anything goes spot.

Inside, Red grabbed a porcelain plate, straight edge razor, and some plastic sandwich bags. He proceeded to walk Quic through the cutting process.

"You grab the razor like this," Red said as he positioned the razor between his thumb and index finger holding it above the boulder at a 90-degree angle. "Using the tip of the blade gives you a clean cut that produces little crumbs. The less crumbs, the better."

Red was an expert at cutting. In the end, he'd cut the boulder down to sixteen pebbles. "These are $20 rocks. You should make like $320 off this."

Quic expressed his appreciations, "Good looking Red." He then went to work on the Boulevard. Quic sold all the rocks within three hours. The easy money left him high as the people who used the drugs. He re-upped immediately. Quic wound up hanging out all night. When he finally went home, he had $500 cash and six $20 pebbles. He was officially hooked.

Chapter Five

Rolling

Quic never returned to his job at McDonald's. The grinding labor for distant results lost appeal in the face of a sexy game that gave instant gratification. The decision had been made the night he got his first pay check. There was no turning back. Quic turned matador and took the game by its horns.

The first week was real education with Quic becoming a dedicated student of economics. He attended the University of Wilmington Arms with Dr. Red as his professor. Hustling came easily to Quic. He was a natural. He went from copping quarter ounces to copping whole ounces in under two weeks.

Red was genuinely happy for Quic. He liked to see homies on the come up getting their paper. Of course, he had a self-serving motivation. Red was Quic's supplier. He, therefore, benefitted from every sale that Quic made. Quic was a straight A student who grasped the intricacies of drug dealing economics with ease. He planned to master and manipulate them in his favor at every turn. These thoughts ran through his mind as he wrapped his knuckles across the iron bars that Red had paid to have installed at Gale's apartment.

"Who is it?" Red answered in a voice that said he hadn't been awake to long.

"Quic."

The locks on the wooden door cranked loudly. Red pulled the door inward allowing light to flood the enclosed hall. He then unlocked and opened the bar door. "What up, Cuz?"

"Top of the morning." Quic shook Red's hand before entering.

"Damn, Cuz, what time is it?"

"Like seven. I got school, but I wanted to cop first." Quic had sold out before returning home on the previous night.

"Damn, Cuz, you could have waited 'til after school." Red wiped the sleep from his eye with the tip of his index finger.

Quic took a seat on the black velvet sectional. He pulled the money from his pocket and set it on top of the glass topped coffee table.

Red grabbed the money. "Hold on," he said before disappearing into the bedroom.

When Red returned, he had a zip lock bag full of big chunks that amounted to more than the two ounces Quic was expecting. He also had a triple beam scale.

"How much is all that?" Quic asked curiously.

"Five or six ounces. Why? You want more?" Red smiled.

"Depends."

"It depends," Red chuckled, "What does it depend on?"

"How much it will run me."

"Let's see," Red looked towards the ceiling as if he was calculating numbers. "I'll give you four and a half. I'll keep the G you just gave me, and you can give me the other twelve fifty later."

Quic laughed. "That ain't no deal Red. If I buy that I'll be just sitting on dope for the hell of it." He paused then continued "How much you copping Red? Like a bird or two?"

Red laughed. He was copping much more than that, but that wasn't Quic's business. "Why?"

"Whatever it is you are not paying five hundred an ounce. The more you cop, the cheaper you get it. Business 101. We spend ten cents for a pack of Now-a-Laters at Miracle Market. If we go to Smart & Final's and get the big box, we end up paying like five cents a pack." Quic smiled. He was proud of himself.

Red laughed. He couldn't help but admire Quic's come back. "What do you think would be a fair price?"

Quic took a page from Red's book and looked toward the ceiling as if he was calculating numbers.

Red told Quic to think about it for a minute while he excused himself. Quic was cool with it. He knew that Red was taking a trip to the kitchen to get some of the food that consisted of nostril titillating bacon.

Red returned holding two porcelain plates with crisp brown bacon, scrambled eggs, and golden biscuits. "Here you go, homie." He handed one to Quic.

Quic stomach growled before he could respond. He tried to cough to cover it up.

"Thanks, homie."

"Don't trip."

Quic and Red dug into their meals. Between bites, Quic made his move, "I'll give you two G's."

Red remained quiet, Quic could not tell if the food or the price was responsible. Quic decided to wait it out. He finished off his food while he waited.

Red emptied his plate then wiped his mouth with the back of his hand. "Look, Cuz, I'm gonna do you one better. Give me eighteen five. You can still give me the other on the back end."

"Huuh, eighteen five now and the rest on the back end?"

"Nah. Eighteen five all together. The G you just gave me and the other eight fifty later."

"Oh, Oh Ok. I got the other eight fifty now. You can walk to the back with me and grab it now."

"I ain't trippin'," Red said in full lazy mode. The meal he'd just devoured had him feeling super heavy.

"I would prefer to give it to you now. I like doing my business straight up. I don't like owing people. It ain't personal."

"Ahight, hold on for a sec." Red respected where Quic was coming from. He wasn't leaving the house without washing up though.

He had Quic wait for five minutes while he washed his face and brushed his teeth. When he was done, he donned a black Compton baseball cap and went with Quic.

●●●

Lil Jay was surprised to learn that Quic had started selling dope. He didn't hate on Quic; He just never thought that Quic would sell dope. Quic was talented as fuck. He was good enough for the pros. Quic was destined to be the hood success story. He was gonna ride his talents to the NBA. He was gonna be rich the legit way.

Lil Jay loved basketball himself. However, he was realistic in knowing that his talent level was nowhere near Quic's. He wasn't tripping though. He was a hood nigga through and through. He loved Park Village more than he loved basketball, so it was all good.

Lil Jay wasn't the most conscious individual, but it didn't take Malcom X intelligence to know that the deck was stacked against him and those who were from where he was from.

Quic's becoming a hustler brought him and Lil Jay closer. They became nearly inseparable. They went to school together. They attended basketball practice together. They hugged the block hustling together. They dated girls who were friends. Well, it was something like that.

Quic saw Tracy a lot, but he still hadn't been able to shake the cool male friend thing yet. He was hell bent on changing this though. He just needed to figure out how to go about doing it.

Quic and Lil Jay took Brenda and Tracy to the Alondra Six to check out Eddie Murphy's Harlem Nights. Quic planned to change the way Tracy looked at him on this date. He had gone as far as seeking advice from Red on how to do this.

Red had not provided any jaw dropping information or anything. He simply advised Quic to get at the girl with the real. That is exactly what Quic planned to do. Quic gave himself a pep talk that left him big basketball game motivated. Tracy would be his before the night was over.

Tracy didn't help any. She started talking about her statutory rapist of a boyfriend as soon as she and Quic were seated in the theater. Lou Dog apparently beat the hell out of her because he thought that she was cheating with someone her own age.

Quic listened attentively and offered an occasional understanding nod. He felt sorry for Tracy more than he wanted to get with her at this moment. Still, he did want to get with her.

"Check this out, Cuz. Ma nigga like you, girl. He ain't tryin' to hear all that bullshit about that no-good as old dude you fuckin' wit." Lil Jay spoke up for Quic.

"Excuse you?"

"No excuse you. Ma nigga ain't spendin' his money on you to sit here and listen to you talk about some other nigga. What you think this is an Oprah special or something?"

Tracy's mouth hung open for a sec before she started to defend herself. "It, it ain't like that. Quic da don't even like me like that. Ya you don't know what you are talkin' about."

Lil Jay balled his face up then looked at Quic. "Cuz, get at this bitch. Tell her ass what's up."

Quic was embarrassed as hell, but he also was cool with Lil Jay getting his back. Plus, what Jay was saying was the truth. One side of Quic wanted to laugh while the other side wanted to run and hide.

"Do you feel that way, Quic?" Tracy wanted to know.

"What way?" Quic said.

"The way he's talking about." Tracy flipped her head in Lil Jay direction.

Quic drew a blank. Thoughts eluded him. This was his chance. The chance he'd envisioned, albeit not under the given circumstances.

Lil Jay had spoken Quic's truth. A truth that Quic himself had failed to speak. Had Quic spoken this truth now he would have looked like an insensitive jerk.

"Well?" Tracy interrupted the silence that Quic failed to end.

"Get at her, Cuz." Lil Jay got on Quic.

"Get out they business, nigga." Brenda was tired of Lil Jay pressing her girl.

"Hold on, hold on," Quic cleared his throat. "Look, Tracy, I'm good with being there for you. I'm not asking you to be a nigga girl or nothing, but on the real, you kinda get at a nigga like he gay or somethin'. You come around lookin' all good and shit," He paused and looked at the exposed cleavage of Tracy's double D's. "Then get ta talking about the old dude. Do I like you? I'm not sure you ain't really given me a chance to. Do I think you are sexy? Will I get with you? Hell yea. You sexy as fuck. Though I am not really trippin', I would definitely fuck with you."

A smile had crept across Tracy's face while Quic was talking. Though she was surprised by his words, she apparently liked what he'd said. She was so caught up in the moment that she didn't even notice when Quic had stopped speaking. Quic may have taken the scenic route but, in the end, he accomplished what he had set out to accomplish.

Tracy did not have sex with Quic that night, but she did express a desire to continue kicking it with him. She also assured him that she never thought he was gay. "I just thought that you did not like me," she told him.

Quic was cool with this. At the end of the date when he and Lil jay dropped the girls off, Quic went for the gusto and did not get disappointed. He kissed Tracy for the first time, a long, wet, and sloppy tongue kiss.

Chapter Six

The Tee Zone

The Tarbabe's ran off four more victories following their defeat of Centennial. This left them one win away from the double-digit win margin, something the school had not accomplished in over five years.

Quic, averaging 15 points, 11 assists, five rebounds, and seven steals, was doing his thing. His financial hustle was good as well. Aside from a few odds and ends purchases that included twin pairs of North Carolina inspired Jordan's for him and his baby brother Mark, Quic stacked. He was also handling his business with the ladies. Though he didn't have a bona fide girlfriend, he'd been steadily courting two.

Tracy, thanks to Lil Jay, knew that Quic wanted more than a friendship with her. With Tasha, it wasn't exactly clear yet, as timing had not allowed him an opportunity to make his move.

Quic wasn't a virgin nor was he afraid of girls. Once he got past that initial bout of shyness Quic morphed into a cold little Don Juan.

Girls found Quic to be cute in a nerdy non-bad boy way. He sported a tapered fade and dressed in Guess jeans cross cords, and used jeans most of the time. He owned khakis but rarely wore them. He courageously followed his idol Michael Jordan in wearing diamond studs in both ears. This was a no-no with antiquated thinking hood cats of the time. It wasn't a strong enough display of machismo.

Tasha's situation was like Tracy's in that she too had been abused by previous boyfriends. Quic assumed that Tasha's abuse had been purely verbal. Tasha had three brothers that were all active blood gang members who had reputations for handling their business, especially Big Indo an OG, who through selling weed by the same name had long paper.

Quic considered Tasha number one girl material, though from the hood Tasha wasn't the average home girl. She was a dime with a banging body, but that wasn't it. She was also highly intelligent. Tasha was an honor student at Lynwood High School. She was a culturally conscious young lady who planned to engage the historically black college experience. She would definitely get a scholarship.

Quic having taken the luxury of including NBA stardom in his future thought that he should find someone who had the potential to be a good wife early on. He wanted someone who would want him for him not who he was destined to become.

Quic was knocked out sleep early Saturday morning when his mother burst through his bedroom door, "Michael," she placed her hand on his bare shoulder and shook him awake.

"Huh, huh" he stirred awake rubbing his eyelids with the backs of his hands.

"Telephone, baby." Quic's mother was a caramel beauty who, having had him at a young 14, looked more like his sister. She handed him the old school push button phone attached to the long cord designed for travel around the entire house.

"Hello," he said. Quic's voice was gruff denoting the hot breath giving chase.

"Hey, you," the sweet voice on the other end sang.

Quic didn't have to ask who was on the other end. Tasha was the only person that Mrs. Green would wake him up for. Mrs. Green loved Tasha. She remembered Tasha from the youth action center days.

Tasha had recited Maya Angelou's "I Rise" poem and had given a speech dealing with self-accountability in a sea of genocidal oppression at a banquet Mrs. Green attended. Mrs. Green believed in her son's NBA potential and was sure he would be successful. She thought that Tasha was a good girlfriend for him.

"What's up, Tee?" Quic lifted himself to a sitting position.

"What's up, sleepy head?"

"Shit, got in late as hell."

"I bet you did." Tasha exhaled loudly.

Quic had told Tasha that he quit his job at McDonald's after being shot at by the Pirus while walking home. He placed the blame squarely on this. The truth would be embarrassing. Tasha would be thoroughly disappointed in him. Quic's worries were in vain as Tasha having grown up around this stuff already knew. She just prayed that Quic's drug dealing was a temporary aberration.

Quic put Tasha on hold while he brushed his grill and took a wiz. When he returned, the two jumped into easy conversation. Quic was a good listener who spent a good portion of the conversation saying, "Yes, um hmm, for real, and I feel you," until he heard something that caught him off guard. "What did you say? Did you say he hit you?"

Tasha did not immediately respond. She waited a few seconds before whispering a barely audible, "Yes."

"Hell nah, how did he get away with that? Big Indo, June Bug, and Um Um Um what's your other brother's name?" Quic closed his eyes and clenched his fist.

"Rick."

"Yea, yea, yea, that's his name. How did that fool get away with that shit?"

"They don't know."

"That's crazy, Tee. You should tell them." Quic was beginning to hate women beaters. That shit to him was so cowardly.

"If I tell them they would go after him. They may get him or they may not. Shit, he has homies, and they have guns. That would be more black-on-black violence that may get my brothers or other families hurt. I don't condone that. I can't be a part of nothing like that," Tasha said in a soft voice.

Tasha was right. Quic knew she was, but the thought of Motoroil getting away with putting his hands on Tasha stirred something deep in him. Perhaps it was the fact that Motoroil had put his hands on him during the game between Compton and Centennial.

"What did I do when that fool pushed me to the ground?" Quic asked himself. "Not a goddamn thing." At that moment, Quic realized that he had no right to question Tasha not telling her brothers.

Tasha, the Nubian princess, became even more attractive to Quic. He wanted her, and she had absolutely no idea.

"Is something wrong with me?" Tasha asked on cue. Like she'd been reading Quic's thoughts.

"Hell no. That shit ain't yo fault." Quic's thoughts went straight to the classic battered women's syndrome, the tactical homicide of the self-esteem. He could not have been more wrong.

"No, no, no. I'm not talking about that. I'm talking about something else."

"Something else?" Quic was lost.

"Yea."

"What?"

"We talk every night and even sometimes in the day time. We've known one another for a long time. You know that I like you, yet you have never tried to get at me."

Quic shot to his feet. It was a good thing he was on the phone and not in person. A cat jumped into his mouth rendering him breathless. "Ha, ha, ha." Was all he could get out.

Quic not only liked Tasha, but he was also secretly obsessed with the thought of Tasha being his girl. Quic's only problem was that he was shy and inexperienced.

"I, I, I la- like you." Quic cringed at the bumbling words he'd embarrassingly released. He covered his mouth with his palm as if trying to push the words back.

"Ah, ah, ah, ma mean ah, I wanna get at you. Ah, ah mean it ain't like that." The words rushed forward as if Quic was trying to get them out before Tasha had a chance to respond.

"Boy, what's wrong with you?" Tasha laughed despite herself.

Quic took a deep breath allowing him a moment to contemplate. "Look, Tasha, I do like you. Shit, I been liking you since we first met at the youth action center, back when you were messing with that dude Blue. I never got at you because you always had a boyfriend. Shit, to be honest, I didn't think I was your type. You always mess with gang bangers. You know gang banging ain't my thing. Nigga ain't in to getting shot down."

"I don't mess with all gang bangers." Tasha knew that her statement wasn't true when she released it. It was partially true in that she'd previously preferred the bad boy thing. This wasn't the case anymore though. Her experience with Motoroil had changed everything.

Tasha and Quic talked for a couple more hours. By the end of the conversation, the two were officially a couple. Quic was happy as hell. He'd hit the lottery. Things were looking good for him.

Chapter Seven

World on Wheels

Quic stood on the boulevard staring into the cloudy sky while sipping strawberry soda through the straw protruding the plastic lid of a Styrofoam cup. He was lost in thoughts of the last conversation he'd had with Tasha. He could not understand how with three reputable gang banging brothers Tasha could still be a victim of abuse. Tasha's beautiful face did not seem the likely canvas for a violent abstract. This and the fact that Tasha had found Motoroil's ugly ass to be boyfriend material confounded Quic. The dude was as attractive as a bamboo's backside.

The screeching scream of a wounded horn snatched Quic from his thoughts. It was dirty Ed in his off-white Riviera. "Quic!" he called.

Quic walked over and pushed his head into the passenger's window, "What's up with you, Ed?"

"Let me get a nick, Big Dog." Ed licked his heavily chapped lips before running his oil-stained mechanic's hand across his ashen face.

Quic dug in the right pocket of his tan khakis and retrieved a dove, "Today is your lucky day. I am in a good mood." Quic handed Ed the whole rock.

Ed's blood shot eyes went wide as he smiled revealing rotten teeth covered in gold leaf, "Thank you, man. Good lookin'."

With the rock secure in the clenched grip of his right hand, Ed fished in his left pocket for the money. The jingles of coins caused Quic's eyebrows to rise putting him on alert. Quic's bull shit-o-meter went crazy.

"Here you go, homie." Ed handed Quic a fist full of change.

Quic rolled his eyes and raised one top of his upper lip, "How much is this, Ed?"

"Ah, ah, ahma be honest wit you, Quic It's like fo' sumthin'."

"What!" Quic scowled, "You said a nick, not no damn four somethin'."

Quic counted the change for himself. It was three dollars and forty-six cents. With angry daggers burning holes through Ed, Quic spoke in an elevated voice, "Give me ma shit back."

"All come on, Quic. Ahm sorry, man. I thought it was five. Come on big dog, look out fo yo boy."

"Fuck that, Ed. You on some bull shit. You should have kept it real from the jump. I wouldn't be trippin', but you tryna play a mothafucka."

"Nah big dog it ain't like that." Ed flashed sad eyes like a kid desperate to get his way. "Please, man, ah need to get this funky mothafucka off ma back. Come on, Quic. Please, man. Ah, ah, ah, I will get it to you. You got ma word."

"Yo word?"

"Yea, baby, ahm a man of ma word. You know me." Ed let out a guttural laugh that was chased by a foul stench.

Quic jumped backwards removing his head from the window. "Damn!"

Ed's pleas tugged at Quic's heart strings. Quic had never used drugs of any kind; however, he was aware of the fact that they had an addictive aspect that left users craving. Quic knew that drug addicts experienced withdrawals when they didn't have their drugs. He was moved by the fact that Ed at forty years of age allowed himself to be reduced to a whining child. Quic wanted to give in, but he was also intimate with the games drug heads played to get what they wanted. He had no desire to be played and, therefore, decided to stick to his guns. He had to; after all, he had been willing to look out for the dude. This was evidenced in Quic's giving Ed the fat dove in the first place.

"Give my shit back," Quic pushed his open palm through the window.

"Hold on, Quic," Ed parked and got out of the car. Quic looked at Ed like he was crazy. He briefly considered the crack head losing his mind and trying to do something stupidly drastic. The young Park Villages that were out hustling as well must have thought the same thing as they started in Quic and Ed's direction.

"No, no, no," Ed's words raced out, "I ain't doin' nothing. Just wanna talk to da homie." He spoke as if he was a Park Village Crip.

Quic laughed. "It's cool. He secretly felt good about the instant backup. He'd known it was there, but seeing it in motion felt amazing.

Ed waited on the fella's retreat and then spoke so rapidly Quic couldn't understand a word he'd said. "Idon'tworktonightwannarentthecar?"

"Slow down, man. What the fuck did you say?"

"Ah don't work tonight. Do you want to use my car?"

This was unfamiliar territory for Quic. He'd never rented a smoker's car before. He knew people who had, but he had never asked about the details. He hadn't even thought about renting a car. The ideal had appeal though. He could go visit his girl amongst other things. "How much?"

"Give me a fat five o, and you can keep it 'til tomorrow."

"Okay, that will work." Quic reached in his stash and got another large dove and an additional dime. "Here."

Ed wanted to kick his own ass. He'd spoken to fast. Quic's immediate agreement told him that he could have gotten more. He'd fucked up, but it was all good. He accepted the rocks. Business was business.

Quic was back in a good mood. He gave Ed an additional dove on the strength. He even offered to give Ed a ride where ever he needed to go. Ed declined; there was no way he could go home without his car. He would have to smoke his dope in a vacant apartment while enjoying the company of a strawberry who, if he wasn't careful, would rob him.

There would be no more hustling. Quic closed shop jumped into the Riviera and got into traffic. Rob's car wash would be his first stop. The Riviera was filthy.

From the car wash, Quic headed straight for Tasha's. Tasha stayed around the corner from the Compton Fashion Center on Killen Street in Mob territory.

Tasha's neighborhood seemed to be in a different Compton than the Wilmington Arms was in. The houses were nice. There weren't any hood insignias spray painted on gates or garages. Had Tasha never said anything, Quic would never have guessed that there was a gang in her neighborhood.

Tasha's house was white with black trim and looked expensive. The lawn was manicured to a perfection that made Quic super conscious about crossing it. He tip-toed across careful not to disturb anything.

Quic thought about his home. Almost every apartment had some form of PVCC spray painted on it. At night, the Wilmington Arms resembled a scene from "Escape from New York," overturned cars, burning trash cans and quartets humming tunes while sipping bottom of the barrel wine. The thoughts nearly overwhelmed him. He would get his family out. He had to. He loved the community and his friends, but he wanted more. He needed more.

The front door to Tasha's house swung inwards at Quic's approach. "Hey, you," Tasha called out before opening the dark gated door. The neighborhood may have looked good, but Tasha's family still opted for double door protection.

Tasha stepped out looking gorgeous in perfectly fitting black jeans that accentuated her shapely hips and a tan long sleeved turtle neck that snuggled her ample breast.

"Damn," Quic exclaimed through an open nearly drooling mouth.

"What are you talking about boy? And why are you walking like that?"

"Huh, ah, shit, I gotta keep it real. You lookin' good as hell right now." Quic hit Tasha with a player smile as if he was shooting cap when he was honest.

"Boy," Tasha recoiled while lowering her head to conceal the awkward smile that appeared across her beautiful mouth.

"Fa-real."

"Why are you walkin' like that?" Tasha wanted to get the attention off her.

"Like what?" Quic had no idea what Tasha was talking about."

"You look like your feet are hurting."

Quic laughed. He hadn't realized that his tentativeness was noticeable. "Ain't nothin' wrong with me. I just don't want to trample y'all bomb ass yard." Quic seemed to be joking, but he was dead serious.

"Boy, please," Tasha chuckled.

"You don't live in escape from New York."

"You don't either."

"Shit, when is the last time you visited the Wilmington Arms?" Quic asked her.

"Never."

Quic hadn't invited Tasha to his stomping grounds for multiple reasons. The main reason being that him not having his own car would render him powerless to control the situation. He'd hate to have to walk Tasha through hustle alley (the boulevard) to the bus stop on Laurel and Wilmington, which was also a dangerous spot. The Park Village Crips had several enemies who would love to catch someone, member or not, slipping.

Quic and Tasha went to Chico's and got a large pepperoni and sausage pizza with extra pepperoni, sausage, and cheese. With the pizza steaming and warm they went to the Rosecrans drive in. The two had a fun time watching Spikes Lee's "Do the Right Thing." Quic was a straight up gentleman. He catered to Tasha's every need and did not try any funny business.

Tasha wasn't disappointed. She did, however, want him to be a little more assertive in the spooning area. Overall though, she had enjoyed herself. The date left her feeling that she could fall for Quic.

Quic had already fallen for her. He had wanted to push the envelope but felt that it would be better to bide his time and do it right. The night and the freedom that came with it left Quic wanting his own car. He'd be renting the Riviera again.

Chapter Eight

King of the Hill

The Tarbabes entered their second game against the Dons having won ten in a row. They were steaming forward impressively. They went in believing that they had to win as respect and city superiority was on the line.

The Dons were on a six-game winning streak of their own. All six wins had been blow outs that led the city's basketball enthusiast to proclaim that they were once again the team to beat. With both teams on fire and wearing chips on their respective shoulders, the game promised to be a thriller of Lakers Celtics proportions.

Quic had been getting his ball on during the streak, but he wasn't doing it alone. Lil Jay averaging an impressive 27 points a game while shooting a lights-out 65 percent from the field was getting his money as well. Also, the team was playing shut down defense.

On the other side, the Dons legitimate 7-foot center Darrell (The Beast) Jackson was drawing Wilt Chamberlin, Kareem Abdul-Jabbar comparisons. With his man amongst boys plays, the seventeen-year-old kid averaged 30 points, 15 rebounds, and seven blocks a game. Darrell drew double and triple teams every time he touched the ball. This freed their perimeter players up for uncontested jumpers. The seemingly dead eyed shooters cashed in. Opponents had no chance. At least, that's what conventional wisdom said.

Coach White, having studied plenty of film, planned to be anything but conventional. He examined local print media in search of predictions. He was confident that predictions would not be favorable for his team. He found several that seemed handpicked for the Tarbabes bulletin board. One predicted a Dons blow-out with their star scoring 50 points while snagging 20 rebounds and ten blocks.

After going over a game plan that simplistically instructed team members to play man to man defense with few if any double teams, coach issued a challenge. With the 50-point prediction plastered boldly on the locker rooms wall, he hollered in a hoarse voice, "If we keep this bum under 20 points, 15 rebounds, and seven blocks, win or lose I will treat you all to a barbeque at my house."

The team, nursing a healthy belief in themselves at this point, readily accepted the challenge. Its confidence soared above the clouds. The young men were jacked to the point that losing was not an option.

Quic listened to Ice T's "Six in the Morning" through the headphones of the brand new Walkman he'd treated himself to while dressing in front of the visiting locker assigned to him. This was a pre-game ritual he'd stolen from the NBA.

Coach White instructed Quic to be purer point guard against the Dons. He wanted him to focus more on being a general and playing shut down defense.

Coach White had coached against the Dons coach for the past five years. He knew that the Dons' coach was a committed counter puncher who loved to study film. Quic had been a shoot first point guard who relied heavily on his superior speed all season. The Dons game plan would thus center on shutting Quic down and daring others to score. Coach White's change in strategy was a chess move.

It was game time. Quic removed his headphones ready for action. Coach gave an emotional pre-game speech that left his troops ready for battle. The Tarbabes hit the hardwood hyped.

The Dons' home court was an entirely different experience than at Compton High School. Every single seat was full. People were standing where there weren't any seats. Red, black, gold, and white flagged like gang colors. The fans were loud, rowdy, and supportive. It was a collegiate atmosphere.

Quic was in awe. This was the way he wanted the Tarbabes home court to be. He planned to do his part to get it this way.

The game started just as coach White had predicted. The Dons' sole focus was on Quic. They full pressed the inbound. When the ball made its way to Quic, they trapped. Quic was unmoved. He passed out of traps and used his speed to get open. He drove and dished every opportunity he got. This worked to perfection as Lil Jay and small forward Erick Daniels camped out behind the arch and hit every shot they took.

The Dons' strategy failed miserably. They fell behind by ten within the first three minutes of the game. The coach called the press and traps off, but it was too late. The damage had been done.

The Tarbabes ran with the lead. They never looked back. The game wound up being a lop-sided blowout. The Tarbabes proved that they were the real deal.

When the Tarbabes left Dominguez, they were on a drug addict's first high. They were the show time Lakers walking with the swagger of champions. The team praised Quic. Erick took it a step further, "We gonna change your name to Air Swag."

Quic's smile dropped, and his eyes narrowed, "Nah, homie, my name is Quic."

Erick was taken aback. He had not intended to offend his friend. He didn't understand. He'd thought that he was giving Quic props.

Lil Jay cleared his throat before stepping in, "A, Erick, the homie's dad gave him his name."

"Oh, oh, shit I didn't know," Erick looked in the distance as Quic's response now made sense. Nothing else needed to be said. Quic's dad, whom he'd been close to, had passed away years before. Quic's name and a few pictures were all that he had left to remember his dad. It was a sensitive issue.

Erick put his hand on Quic's shoulder, "My bad, homie. I didn't know."

"Ah know. It's all good."

Quic's dad had been a stand out high school athlete who'd earned scholarships in basketball, baseball, and track. He had been Compton's own Jim Brown.

Quic's dad was also a first-generation Crip. His commitment to Crip would ultimately derail his athletic pursuits in a way that landed him the label of the Pee Wee Kirkland of Compton.

Though Quic's dad, whose gang name had been Bay Rob, lost his sports dreams to gang banging he did not go all bad. Having started banging at a young fifteen, his career lasted all of five years. He stopped banging after his first, and only, prison bid.

Two months into a two-year bid Bay Rob became a dad for the first time. Ms. Smith, who would later become Mrs. Green, gave birth to Quic.

Mrs. Green was head over heels in love with Bay Rob. She wanted her son to be his junior, but Bay Rob whose birth name was Robert Green wasn't having it. He'd tarnished his name when he allowed his Crip affiliations to fuck up his athletic career. His son deserved better. He deserved a fresh start with a clean slate; Bay Rob would give it to him.

Bay Rob's son was destined for greatness. He, therefore, would name him for such. A young Michael Jordan had taken the NBA by storm and was tearing things up. Then there was Michael Jackson, the unchallenged king of pop. That was it, Michael, Michael Green. Yes, that was it, another Michael destined for greatness.

From that moment forward, Bay Rob became Robert Green again, a strong black man, a committed father, and when the opportunity presented itself the world's greatest husband.

Quic and his mom never visited Mr. Green while he was locked up. Quic's mom was underage. Mr. Green made up for missed time when he got out of prison. He spent as much time as humanly possible with his son. He taught Quic how to play sports.

By the time Quic reached ten, it was apparent that he was athletically gifted. He had the speed of an adult. His dad used to take him to east Compton Park, home of the tennis court where Richard Williams trained Venus and Serena and allow him to race all comers.

People who had known Mr. Green from his athletic days dubbed Quic his dad's junior and took to calling him Speedy, an old sports name Mr. Green once carried. Mr. Green, once again wanting to separate his son from his failed past, promptly nixed the title. He chose instead to call his son Quic. The unconsciously entrenched Crip in Mr. Green would be responsible for the spelling.

The Tarbabes continued with what had become their winning ritual by going to Chico's for pizza and video games. They chilled for a couple hours before going their separate ways.

Brenda and Tracy had attended the game. They'd gone to Chico's as well and had stayed with Lil Jay and Quic when the players went their separate ways.

Quic and Tracy sat in the back seat of Lil Jay's Impala cuddled up while Lil Jay drove the couples down Rosecrans headed for Playa Del Rey. There was no confusion for Quic and Tracy this time around. Quic was a superstar, and she was to be his conquest. Quic smiled to himself.

When the couples got to the beach, it became apparent that the cold would not allow for a comfortable trip. The couples made the joint decision to take the party to the Best Western. It was going down, no ifs, ands, or supposes. It was long overdue.

The girls stayed in the car while Quic and Lil Jay rented the rooms. "Cuz, you betta tear dat ass up. Pay her ass back for thinkin' she could talk yo ear off about some otha nigga." Lil Jay smiled from ear to ear as if it was him who was getting ready to have sex with Tracy.

"Don't worry about nothin'. That ass is mines. She ain't gone have shit else to say about yo boy after this."

In the room, Quic wasted no time getting Tracy out of her 501's, Tarbabes sweatshirt and Nike Cortez. Foreplay for the young man with limited experience consisted mainly of lip and tongue service to Tracy's neck, chest, and breast. His hands simultaneously explored her curves.

Tracy's caramel twin peaks topped with dark chocolate Hershey kisses turned Quic on something fierce. He licked, sucked and massaged until moistness with an unflattering taste stopped him. His head snapped back like his tongue had encountered the tip of a nine-volt battery.

Tracy's body tensed. She'd felt him pulled away, but had no idea why he'd done it. Her unspecified insecurities stood on standby.

Quic recomposed himself and went back to work, careful not to suck on the Hershey kisses. The sexual opportunity was not going to pass him by; not on this night.

With the two laid across the soft quilted queen size bed, Quic fisted his love tool while lining it in preparation for entry. Tracy purred.

Tracy received Quic warmly. Her warmness invited Quic with a gentle massaging motion; sending chills through his body that provided a pleasant sensation. She was warm, wet, and heavenly.

Instant gratification threatened to turn Quic into a half-a-minute brother, a terrifying thought indeed. He paused and lay completely still, willing gratification away. Quic wanted to climb the coveted stairway to the promise land just not so soon. His reputation was at stake.

When sensation lay dormant, Quic went back to work. Gratification, that deceitful possum took hold of him within seconds. The unexpected return rendered Quic powerless, with shaking legs and rolling eyes he gave in.

When it was over Quic lay on top of Tracy quietly looking towards round two. Despite his having only rented the room for an hour, there had to be a round two. It would have to be a quick turn around, but it had to happen.

Round two proved a duplicate of round one. Quic had no answers. He quietly basked in confusion throughout the couples' drive back to Compton.

Chapter Nine

Seduced

Ed's Riviera became the Cleopatra to Quic's Julius Caesar. The power of the 350, the tranquility when cruising the highway accompanied by soothing tunes, the freedom to get in traffic at will all had Quic hooked. He wanted in.

Renting the Riviera every possible opportunity over the past three weeks had taken an economic toll. Quic knew that if he continued renting it, he would wind up paying the Rivieras purchase price several times over. He needed to buy a car for himself.

Quic broached the subject with Red when he went to re-up. "A, homie, do you know where I can get a ride for a decent price?"

"I don't know, homie. I ain't into that shit. I don't need one. Shit, you see I don't even barely leave the hood." Red said seriously.

"Okay, good lookin' anyway."

"Don't trip. A whatever happened with old girl from Palmer? Did you ever get that?"

Quic smiled, "Yeah, I cracked her."

"Did you hit?"

Quic's smile disappeared at the thought of his less than stellar performance. His answer was a simple, "Yeah."

"Damn, Cuz, was it that bad?" Red laughed.

Quic couldn't tell Red what he really thought, so he took an alternative route, "Nah, it was cool. A, let me ask you something. What is it when you sucking a girl's titties and some moist shit with a sour taste come out?"

Red burst out laughing. "That tha ha ha That's breast milk. Baby lactating. Did she just have a baby?"

"Nah, not that I know of. Nah hell nah. I would know that."

"She must be pregnant or somethin'. That shit is associated with kids."

"Oh shit, oh, oh, okay." Quic smile returned as the situation suddenly became clear to him.

Tracy was pregnant. She had to be. He'd never had sex with a pregnant girl before. However, he had heard a gang of stories about the experience. He'd heard that the pregnant girl's love is always warm, wet, and thoroughly inviting. That was exactly what Tracy had been. Just thinking about it made him want to explode. The conversation with Red left Quic feeling a lot better about his performance with Tracy. He had a legitimate excuse.

The good feeling was short lived. Though having an excuse was cool Tracy's being pregnant meant that in having sex with her he had entered a sacred place that housed a tiny human, a tiny human life that wasn't his. He'd cum in that place, on the head of another man's child. It felt inappropriate. Though Quic left Red with confused emotions, he still nursed a stomach-knotting desire for the lovely Cleopatra. He went to Lil Jay's in search of assistance.

Lil Jay was at the kitchen table eating Frosted Flakes. "What up, Cuz?" he called while chewing sloppily.

"Shit, I'm thinkin' about buying a car. You know where I can get one for cheap?"

Cereal followed by a throaty laugh leapt from Jay's mouth, "Yo ass done got sprung on that rental."

"Hell yea, man. That shit done got me."

"That shit always happens to niggas. Cars are like cold-hearted bitches with bomb ass pussy."

Quic wasn't sure what Lil Jay was talking about, but he went with it. He simply wanted Jay to help him find a car.

"I got my shit out the 'Recycler.'" Lil Jay said after wiping his mouth with the back of his hand.

"What is that?"

"It's a newspaper-like magazine where people take out ads to sale their cars. A new one comes out every week.

"Where can I get one?"

"Miracle Market. Hold on. Let me clean up. I'll take you up there."

After brushing his teeth, Lil Jay stashed the work that Quic had just coped from Red and drove the single block to the neighborhood liquor store and mini market that sat directly across the street from Louisiana Fried Chicken.

When Lil Jay and Quic returned to the Wilmington Arms, they were greeted by the window rattling sound of Ice Cubes "Gangster Gangster." Their older homie Lorenzo's car, a show-ready metallic blue candy 1961 Impala with blue fade aways sitting on chrome Dayton's with the metallic eagles, was parked in front of Lil Jay's apartment.

Lil Jay bopped his head to the beat and with a smile on his face asked Quic, "You looking for something like that?"

"Nah, nothing like that." Quic's expression was grave; he had not caught the joke.

The two best friends took the "Recycler" inside of Lil Jay's house and began their search. After looking through the entire

"Recycler" Quic was interested in three cars. There had been plenty Impalas, Old's mobiles, Regals, and Monte Carlos but everyone had those though. Quic had no desire to be like everyone.

Quic had chosen a Capri and two Mazda RX7s. The Capri was advertised for $900 while the RX7s were advertised for $1100 and $800 respectively. After test drives and a spirited negotiation process, Quic bought the $800 RX7 for $600. It was nice, a midnight blue paint with no dents or scratches. The engine purred quietly, and the car drove smoothly. It was a steal that left Quic extremely happy.

Lil Jay had taken Quic to the Jordan Downs in Watts to buy the car. He followed Quic back to the Wilmington Arms where he parked his car so he could ride shot gun with Quic. The new car owner had work to do.

The first place Quic and Jay went was to the window tint shop behind Larry's muffler on Long Beach Boulevard next to the Compton Fashion Center. Quic knew the proprietor Big Mike through his uncle Greg who installed car stereo systems in the parking lot of the Compton Fashion Center.

Big Mike sent Quic to the Pep Boys across the street to purchase the tinted paper. He then charged him fifty bucks for installations.

Quic marveled at how easy the process was, as simple as removing a sheet of plastic from the tinted paper, spraying water on the window, applying the tint then smoothing it out with a squeegee. That was it.

Quic's next stop was the Compton Fashion Center. It was time to get uncle Greg to hook him up. Greg was under the dashboard of a White 1964 Impala on 13' Daytons with 520 tires when Quic slapped him on the belly, "What up, Unc?"

Greg peeked from under the dashboard. "What up, Neph? How you been?"

Quic told Greg about the RX7 he'd just bought. "I need some bumps, Unc. I got to do it right. Are you going to hook me up?" Greg readily agreed, "Neph, how much are you working with?"

Quic pulled a knot of bills from his pocket, "Whatever I need."

"Cool, go get an Alpine-dash, two Pioneer six by nines, two Cerwin Vega woofers, one HK amp, and an Alpine pre-app."

Quic did as told. Thirty minutes later he returned ready for his uncle to hook him up. He'd pay him for his services for certain as he respected the hustle. He did, however, expect a family discount.

Everything was going well until a gold 1979 Regal bumping Slick Rick's "Children's Story" pulled up. The sun was descending into dusk while a shivering cold was settling in. Quic stood next to Lil Jay at the rear of the RX7 with his arms folded.

"Damn, Cuz, you see that?" Lil Jay spoke first.

The driver and the passenger of the Regal both sported bright red Philadelphia Philly's baseball caps, loc's and menacing expressions.

Quic nodded his head slowly and said, "Yea." Lil Jay was Quic's best friend, but at this moment Quic really wished that Jay had not come with him.

Quic did not care that the Regal's occupants wore red. He did not care that they were Pirus. If he were by himself when the Pirus hit him up, which he knew they were going to do, he'd only say that he did not gang bang, and that would be it. The fools would keep it pushing. Instead, Quic gritted his teeth while mentally preparing to engage in battle.

Lil Jay tugged at the brim of his Dallas Cowboys cap. The smile he sported had lasted only seconds before it turned into a murderous mask.

The Regal pulled to a screeching stop in front of Quic and Jay blocking the RX7. The green-eyed, high yellow driver stepped out sporting a red sweat shirt, tan khakis, and construction boots with red shoe strings. He was followed by the blue-black complexioned passenger who resembled Motoroil. This short and stocky cat looked like something straight from the pages of a National Geographic book. Another guy came from the back seat of the Regal. This dude caramel complexioned was paper thin. He looked scared as hell but had to ride with his homies.

"What up, blood? What dat Mob like?" The driver was first to speak.

"Fuck slob, Cuz. This Park Village Crip!" Lil Jay's chest pushed out and took the form of a barrel.

"Fuck Crab," the driver started but was cut short by a well-placed over hand right that sent him crashing to the cement.

The National Geographic kid took flight on Lil Jay in his home boy's defense. A solid left sent Lil Jay stumbling backwards. Quic rushed the kid with a flurry of lightning fast blows. The kid took a couple steps backwards to steady himself. He and Quic then locked up like pit bulls.

A few seconds into the rumble the kid from National Geographic fell backwards and was out like a light. Lil Jay after throttling the driver had brought Quic's fight to an end with a blindsided right.

Greg grabbed Quic by the shoulders, "What the fuck y'all doin'? Fuck, man, this is my fucken job. Y'all bringin' that stupid ass gang shit here. Get your fucken friend and get the fuck out of here."

Quic knew that his uncle was right, but his pride and a desire to have his music finished caused him to protest, "I don't care about no gang shit, but them fools fucked with us. This is a free world. Fuck dem dudes. I ain't goin' nowhere to ma music is done." He rested himself out of Greg's grip and stood his ground.

"Look, Neph," Greg's tone softened, "Take your friend inside and go get me some wire. Mr. Chow's the first shop to the right when you go through the side door."

"Come on, Jay, "Quic followed his uncle's directions.

Greg did not gang bang anymore; however, he had once been a Piru from Lime hood. When Quic and Jay were out of sight, Greg helped the young Pirus get themselves together and demanded that they leave and not return. He feared they would come back shooting.

When the driver protested Greg planted seeds of dissension.

"Y'all need to take little scary blood to the hood and beat his ass. He let y'all get whipped on and didn't do shit." What he was doing was wrong, but better the little dude than him or his nephew.

The Pirus got in the car and went about their business. Greg was not convinced that they would not return shooting so he made

Quic and Lil Jay leave. He told them that he would follow them and finish the job in the Wilmington Arms.

Greg did just as he'd said he would. Quic's music was installed and bumping by eight that night. Quic was in the game. In one day, he brought and hooked up a car. It was on.

Chapter Ten

Red Dawn

Quic was up early Saturday morning. Whether it was an early morning or late night was debatable as he was on the heels of an all-nighter where he played hustler/taxi driver. Quic knew that he needed to make some of the money he'd spent back and he also had no desire to let the precious leave his sight. He volunteered to make all late-night store runs. He also volunteered to give the homies who no longer lived in the hood but returned every day without a consistent means of transportation rides to their respective homes.

The RX7 addiction left Quic on a speed high that had him thinking that he did not need sleep. It was just after 8:00 am when he eased through the drive through of the Louis Burger's on Compton Boulevard and Alameda. It was breakfast time. More importantly, he needed to waste a couple hours. Rob's car wash, where he planned to treat his mistress to a full body massage complete with a manicure and pedicure, did not open until 9:00 am.

After ordering the intestinal assault that was chili cheese French fries topped with pastrami to go, Quic parked in front of Rob's and went to work. The Styrofoam tray was tongue licking clean in under ten minutes. He was sipping strawberry soda from an extra-large Styrofoam cup when at 8:30 am Rob made an early arrival.

Rob opened the car wash an immediately started on Quic's car. By 9:30 am, Quic was in traffic looking like he was in a hot ride fresh from the paint shop.

Quic's next stop was AQ's menswear where he purchased an outfit for the day. He went home showered, got dressed, and in under an hour was back in traffic. It was time to introduce his girl to his mistress.

Tasha stood on her front porch looking through wide eyes as Quic pulled to a stop in front of her house. Quic's arrival had been announced by the window rattling base of Dana Dane's

"Cinderfella." Tasha's mouth hung open in surprise. Quic hadn't told her about the RX7. He'd planned to surprise her, and that was exactly what he had done.

Tasha wagged her index finger at Quic and with a smile on her face said, "What the hell?"

Quic turned the music down and cut the engine, "What did you say?"

"That damn music was loud, boy."

Worry crossed Quic expression, "Oh, shit, my bad. Did your mom hear it?"

Eric B and Rakim's "Paid in Full" drowned out Tasha's response.

The gold Regal from the Compton Fashion Center had bent the corner off Bradfield and was pushing up Killen Street.

"Fuck," Quic mumbled. This wasn't good.

Tasha saw the car but didn't think anything of it. It was her brother's homeboy, Smurf. Speeding through the streets of the neighborhood bumping loud music wasn't out of the ordinary for him. He did that every day.

Tasha was, however, shocked when Smurf pulled to a screeching stop in the middle of the street beside Quic. She was even more surprised when Smurf threw the car in park and after exiting said to Quic, "What's hattenin', Blood!"

Quic looked at Smurf with a calm that betrayed his trembling legs. The fact that he did not gang bang didn't mean a thing in this instant. The incident at Compton Fashion Center had branded him a Park Village Crip in Smurf's eyes.

Three additional cars pulled to a screeching stop before Quic could respond. Several occupants exited from the doors. Within seconds, a sea of red stood in front of Quic and Tasha calling out blood chants, "What up, blood? What's hattenin', Blood? Dat Mob like, Blood?" There were so many Blood chants that it started to seem like "blood" was the most dominant word in the English language.

The sight and sound of this made Quic want to turn and run. He was in an impossible position. He had absolutely no win. His ego latching on to the prospect of Tasha's branding him an undesirable coward pushed the thought from his mind.

"What the fuck is this?" Tasha screamed from the top of her lungs while shooting daggers at Smurf.

"Yo nigga is a crab. You know beta than bringing dem crab ass niggas in da hood."

"What?" angry surprise registered across Tasha's face, "What in the fuck are you talking about? Michael doesn't even gang bang."

"That ain't what the nigga said the other day."

The loud click clack of a bullet being slammed into the chamber of a 12-guage riot pump shot gun brought forth a deafening silence. All eyes shot towards Tasha's front porch where her big brother Indo stood looking like a brown skinned predator's Arnold Schwarzenegger freshly paroled from San Quintin. He sported a crisp wife beater along with a menacing expression. "What's hattenin", Blood?" his voice thundered.

Big Indo was ready for war. His massive hands gripped the pistol grip handle of the 12-guage tightly causing the insides of his hands to blanch while every vein in his upper torso protruded. He looked like a jacked body builder.

"What's brackin', Big Indo?" Smurf called out to his big homie.

"I don't know. You tell me. The fuck all you niggas parked in front of ma mothafuckin' house on some gang bang shit fo?"

"Ba Ba, Blood a crab," Smurf pointed at Quic like a kid telling on another kid.

"What?" Indo boomed.

"Yea, blood and his homeboys rushed us at the fashion center the other day."

A puzzled expression crossed Indo's face. He lowered the gage, "What? Blood don't gang bang. That's ma sister's boyfriend. He's a basketball player."

Smurf shook his head in protest, "Nah, on Bloods that's Blood. He was in that car, him and a tall nigga. They was getting they music hooked up."

Indo looked at the RX7 then at Quic, "What is he talkin' about, Quic?"

Quic cleared his throat before speaking. "I don't gang bang. I was at the fashion center though, and I did get into it with dude." He paused to look at Smurf. "It wasn't like he saying though. Him and his homeboys jumped out the car banging on my peoples. My peoples is a Crip from Park Village, and he banged back. The two got into a heads-up fight. Me and some of your other homeboys were watching. My peoples were getting the best of him, so one of his homies jumped in. I don't care about the gang thing, but I couldn't let my peoples get jumped, so I jumped in. The other guy and I went head up, and that was that."

Quic's story, though not entirely accurate, was cool because it didn't expose how the Bloods had gotten throttled two on two while a third sat by and watched. Smurf was cool with that. He did, however, have one contention, "Nah, man you banged Park Village on us."

Quic Looked at Indo with sincere eyes, "I swear to God I did not bang anything on them. I don't care about that banging shit. That's on everything I love."

"This is fucked up. Y'all are so damn disrespectful. You a fuckin' punk, Smurf!" Tasha cried.

"Go in the house, Tasha." Indo was an angry parent now. "Now."

Tasha did as she was told. Indo then sat the gauge just inside the front door. "Get y'all cars out the street before someone call one time."

The other Pirus could see that Indo had the situation under control. They all went about their business. Smurf, however, pulled his car to the curb.

Indo pulled Smurf and Quic to the side. "Look, Smurf, Blood ain't no crab. He don't bang. That's on the Mob. But even if he did bang, he at my house as a guest. Out of respect fo me blood got a pass comin'. You know what time it is. When you bring the homies to my house on some gang bang shit, you disrespectin' me and ma fam. That ain't cool. Dis shit can't happen again. On Bloods. On anotha note, do you got somethin' you wanna get off yo chess with Blood? On Mob, y'all can go in the back yard and handle that shit."

Smurf swallowed a wad of spit then cleared his throat, "Nah, nah, big homie. Ah, ah, ahm cool dats yo people. I will respect that."

Indo laughed. He knew that Smurf was scared. He turned to Quic, "You good?"

Quic wasn't good. He didn't like the stunt that Smurf had pulled, especially because Smurf was obviously afraid. The situation could have gone in a direction that had left Quic in serious peril. However, Quic knew that acting on his displeasure would be a mistake that would make him no better than an average gang banger. "I'm good."

Crisis avoided, Quic took Tasha out for a movie and meal. The remainder of the day went smoothly. Quic couldn't wait to tell Lil Jay what happened. Later that evening when he returned to the

Wilmington Arms he went straight to Jay's house; no one was home. He went to the boulevard. No one was hanging out. This was different. He spotted Tweet the home girl who was strung out on crack walking like a zombie with her head down searching for lost rocks, "A tweet," he called.

"Heyyy, Quic."

"Where is everybody at?"

"Oh, you don't know?"

No, I don't know. If I did would I be asking your stupid ass? Quic thought but decided to say, "No, I don't."

"They at killa king. Lil Jay and Black Tee got shot."

"What? When, where?"

"Ah, ah don't know."

Quic was in full panic mode. He ran full speed to the RX7, hitting the road pushing the pedal to the metal weaving through traffic like Mario Andredi. The short ride seemed to take forever.

The music was bumping, but Quic didn't hear it. His mind drifted back to thoughts of when he and Lil Jay met.

Quic had met Lil Jay, who back then was simply Jeffrey, on the first day of the fifth grade. Quic had just moved to the Wilmington Arms.

Lil Jay was a wanna be at the time. Of course, he had no idea what gang banging was or even meant. He only knew that his uncle Big Ree Bo represented Park Village and was hood royalty. Ree Bo was his idol.

Jay had seen Quic around the ways a couple times. He knew that he was a new resident in the hood but hadn't talked to him. That didn't stop him from hitting him up the first chance he got.

"What up, Cuz? You reppin' the hood or what?"

"Huh?" Quic stood wide eyed with his mouth hanging open. He had no idea what Lil Jay was talking about.

Quic's mom had run a tight ship. She'd lost Quic's father to gang violence. She'd planned to keep her son's as far away from the stuff as possible. It would be years before Quic learned the real story about his dad.

"You bangin' Park Village Crip or what?" Lil Jay displayed the aggressiveness that would later be a staple of his hood persona.

The word Crip caught Quic's attention. There wasn't a kid in the inner city that hadn't heard about the Crips and their accompanying horror stories. Crip was the inner-city boogie man. Quic had been taught to keep his distance

"No, no, I ain't no Crip," Quic responded with an innocence befitting his age.

Lil Jay had been stumped. He didn't know what else to say. He'd only hit Quic up because he'd witnessed Ree Bo do it. No one had ever told Big Ree Bo that they were not banging in Jay's presence.

"You wanna shoot some marbles?" Lil Jay changed courses.

Quic agreed. So, began what would be a lifelong friendship.

Quic parked near the double door emergency entrance of Martin Luther King, Jr. Hospital. He exited the car and power walked to the emergency waiting room where he found Lil Jay and Black Tee's family huddled up with several homies.

Within minutes Quic learned that Lil Jay and Black Tee had made the cardinal mistake of trying to buy liquor at the liquor store on Rosecrans near Willowbrook. The Pirus had noticed Jay's car and came gunning. Black Tee had gotten hit twice in the neck and was in critical condition. Lil Jay had taken two to the leg and would be ok.

Though everything was ok and both homies would eventually pull through Quic was left with a heavy heart. He went home that night and had a long talk with his mom. The discussion concluded with Quic agreeing to go to church with his mom on the following morning.

<u>Chapter Eleven</u>

The Fifth Man

When Quic returned from church with his mom, he was surprised to see that Lil Jay was hobbling around on crutches while choking the neck of a duce duce. The sight was bitter sweet. Lil Jay was alright physically; the cast and crutches were only temporary, they would eventually go away. He would be running, jumping, and even humping (if he wasn't already) in no time. His psychology was a bird of a different feather. A sinister smile on a fractured expression left Jay looking like a distant relative of the Dark Knight's Joker. Lil Jay had the appearance of a walking nightmare poised to wreak havoc.

Quic had to check on his boy. He walked his mom to the front door then took off.

"What up Jay?" Quic approached from the rear.

Lil Jay took a swig before responding. "Shit, ahm here. What's hattenin' wit you? I see you in yo church shit."

Quic chuckled through an exaggerated smile. "Moms was on me. You know how she does it."

"Yea, I Know."

"What's up with you though? How you feelin'? You straight?"

"Yeah, Cuz," Lil Jay leaned against a dusty Thunderbird and sighed like a battle-weary vet. "Ahm straight, straight as fuck. Dem busta mothafuckas can't touch ah Crip. You know?" He paused again. His eyes glossed over as he visited a place in his head available only to him. "Got ma nigga Tee clinging to life. Fuck dem bitch ass niggas on Crip. Nah, fuck Crip on Harry'o."

Lil Jay was serious. Harry'o, a twist on Heroin, was the big homie who'd died after driving his Ninja at over 100 miles per hour through a barred gate into the side wall of a garage while high off PCP. Having been martyred in his mid-twenties Heroin became instant hood royalty. Park Village members put stuff on him to illustrate genuine commitment.

Lil Jay wasn't finished ranting. "Yea, Cuz, I heard them Mob niggas tried to fuck wit you ova Tasha's house. Yeah, don't trip Cuz on PV a mothafucka at dem bitch ass niggas too."

Quic gave pause. Lil Jay was on one. Quic had no desire to fuel the fire; there was no reason to. The situation at Tasha's wasn't that bad. Nobody had been hurt. Hell, nobody even fought.

Quic, therefore, gave a measured response, "Nah, it wasn't like that. It wasn't like that at all. The dude Smurf said something, but Big Indo wasn't having it. He shut him down; told him not to bring that shit to his house. He told Smurf and the rest of their homies that I was off limits. Anyone who wanted to mess with me had to see him. He even told Smurf that he would let the two of us fight head up if Smurf wanted to. I was with it, but dude did not want to see me. That was pretty much it."

Lil Jay squinted his eyes and looked towards the sky, "Which one was Smurf?"

"The one driving the gold Regal. The one you throttled before you came to help me. Good looking out, by the way. I never got a chance to thank you for that."

"Ah fool, you know what time it is," Lil Jay paused to take another swig from his duce duce. He then went on to rage about his enemies. His voice was a mixture of anger, hurt, grief, and sorrow.

Quic quietly listened. He did not interrupt once. Lil Jay needed to get the rage out of his system. When Jay came up for air and beer, Quic jumped in taking an alternative route. "Jay, you know we championship bound. You are our best offensive player, and we need you."

Lil Jay's expression went blank. He looked towards the maroon sky's descending sun, "Quic, I love you, homie. On Park Village Crip, I love da team too. Y'all ma niggas and always will be. I will always see there for y'all. But on some real shit, dis basketball shit is ova fo me. Fuck basketball, homie, this Park Village Crip. I'm all in on dis Crip shit. Dees niggas ain't knowin' dey done woke a sleepin' giant. Dey ain't playing, and neither am I." Jay's war declaration was followed by a single tear. He wiped it away with the back of his hand and took another swig.

Quic didn't speak anymore; neither did Jay. There wasn't anything else to say. The two sat and watched night fall over their Compton world, the Compton world that a rap record could not articulate.

●●●

Tuesday arrived and with it came high school basketball's Thrilla in Manila; Compton's Muhammad Ali vs. Centennial's Joe Frazier.

The Tarbabe's led the division by two games. Though a loss would only make the division race closer, the Tarbabes had no desire to give up the comfort of a two-game cushion. Anything could happen in basketball. Plus, they were without their leading scorer, presumably for the remainder of the season. They needed the win.

Centennial needed the win themselves. They were at home where they hadn't lost a single game in the given season. A lost would crush team morale. Centennial got off to an inspired start hitting eight of their first ten shots and taking an early ten-point lead. Four of the eight made were from beyond the arc.

Coach White was not upset nor did he panic. Lil Jay's replacement Pier Brown played excellent defense. Motoroil just played better offense. Coach White would have like to have his leading scorer, but he wasn't worried that there would be a significant drop off in production from the position. What Pier lacked in experience he more than made up for in pure athletic abilities. Pier's outside shot wasn't as dead eye as Lil Jay's, but it was good. In addition to this, Pier was a deadly slasher who had a killer first step and played shut down defense.

The Apaches cooled off a bit in the second quarter. This coupled with the Tarbabes knocking down a few shots of their own made the game close. The Apaches closed the half out with a modest four-point lead.

Quic hadn't done much at this point in the game. He had nine points and three assists. Still, Coach White wasn't worried. The Tarbabes had Centennial right where they wanted them. Quic would show up for the next half.

During half time Coach White pulled his star to the side and told him that the team needed his leadership. "We need this win for Lil Jay. I know what you said, but I got faith in my little dude. He will be back. We gotta hold it down for him."

Quic agreed with Coach White and committed himself to getting it done.

Quic gave the halftime speech. He spoke from a heavy heart that was laced with emotion. He concluded his speech by getting an ink pen from Coach White and scribbling Lil Jay's number 34 across the tongue of his North Carolina Jordan's and hollering, "For Lil Jay, yaah!"

The entire team roared their agreement and followed Quic's lead in putting Lil Jay's number somewhere on their sneakers and yelling the Park Village call, "Yaah," in unison. The Tarbabes returned to the hardwood sporting serious expressions that signaled they meant business. Led by their star the Tarbabes pressed from the opening inbound. Three quick turnovers and three quick buckets put the Tarbabes ahead for the first time in the game.

The Apaches didn't go away. They too turned it up on defense. The Ali Frazier slug fest turned 90's Heat Knick ugly. The lead swung back and forth several times over the next two quarters. Neither teams lead exceeded four points. In the end, the Tarbabes edged the Apaches by two.

There were no dirty fouls or any fighting this time around. Though both teams still hated one another the slug fest had left all involved with a healthy dose of competitive respect for one another.

The Apache's fans didn't give a damn about competitive respect. They didn't care about respect of any kind. They hated the Tarbabes with a gang banger's passion. They showed this by chasing them from the court with boos and discarded trash.

Thirty minutes after their hard-fought victory the Tarbabes boarded a team bus that had been thoroughly vandalized. Someone had taken a can of red spray paint and scribbled several epithets intended to disrespect Crip gang members and acronyms denoting the culprits various Piru hoods.

The Tarbabes were not surprised. In fact, they'd expected something like this. Their fans had done the same thing to Centennial when they had come to Compton.

Everything was good until the bus driver turned the bus around and headed for the parking lots exit. The chain link fences though open could not be exited. A sea of red sporting teens and young adults blocked the opening. They were loud and excitable. They had no intentions of letting the Tarbabes bus leave unmolested.

The situation suddenly became real. The driver put the bus in reverse before realizing that he had nowhere to go.

Ground vibrating music hushed the crowd; Ice Cube's "Gangster Gangster" rang out. Faces in the crowd turned from the Tarbabes bus to Central Avenue. A flurry of loud pops rang out and played the role of Moses by parting the Red Sea giving way to a hasty exit for the Tarbabes team bus. The driver didn't have a clue as to what had taken place. He didn't even care he was just happy to be out of the situation. The Tarbabes squad, on the other hand, having peeped the Midnight Blue Glasshouse burning rubber away knew exactly what had taken place. They were ecstatic; their leading scorer had come through and saved the day once again.

Chapter Twelve

My Brother's Keeper

The Tarbabes win against Centennial, their 13th in a row, allowed them to lock the division down. Though Pier brown had done an exceptional job in place of Lil Jay, Quic wanted his boy back. The team was not the same without him. They would not be where they were without Lil Jay.

Lil Jay had been a real life wrecking ball since he and Black Tee had gotten shot. He'd become obsessed with not only exacting revenge but with sending the message that Park Village wasn't to be fucked with.

Around this time, Lil Jay's Samoan Homeboy TC had been gunned down by a nearby Mexican gang called Crazy Locos. TC had put hands on one of their reputable homies named Shadow whose name was a product of his dark complexion. TC and Shadow had fought over a girl in front of a sizeable crowd. Shadow's ego would not allow him to accept losing the fight. Two days after the fight Shadow and two of his homie crept through a hole in the gate of the Park Village apartments and gunned TC down, a first and last of its kind.

Park Village members were devastated by the lost. They were livid at the way it had happened. The leaders called a meeting and issued an all-out murderous declaration; Crazy Locos would pay. This was right up Lil Jay's ally, as he was still reeling from his own situation. Lil jay was eager to further his "Park Village ain't to be fucked with" message. The signs were on the wall. Quic could read them clearly. Getting shot had broken Lil Jay. If something didn't change, Lil Jay was headed for an early death or a life sentence. Quic having major love for Lil Jay did not want to see this happen. He decided to stage a one-man intervention. He would get Lil Jay back involved with the team for their playoff run. He would get Jay to workout with him in preparation for the playoffs and in the process, make Jay miss and subsequently want to re-join the team. Basketball would give him a break from the gang banging. It would hopefully bring him back to his senses; it would work. It had to.

Quic found Lil Jay wiping dust from the freshly sprayed baby blue paint that now adorned the glass house. The incident at Centennial necessitated the change.

"Damn, Jay, you still limping. Man, you betta get in a gym and get your strength up," Quic called from behind Lil Jay.

Lil Jay smiled over his shoulder. He then turned around and directed Quic's eyes towards his own waist where a nickel plated .45 semi-automatic pistol rested, "As long as I got my trusty bitch, I'm good."

Quic wanted to remind Lil Jay that his trusty bitch hadn't done anything to save him and Black Tee from what had happened to them a few weeks earlier, but thought better. He shook his head and said, "I feel you, but ain't nothing like haven yo health right."

"I hear you, Cuzin'." Jay went back to wiping the dust from his car.

Quic watched Lil Jay for a contemplative second before deciding to change tactics, "We did it, homie. We turned the team around and locked shit down. We got a realistic chance at State."

Lil Jay spoke without turning around, "Oh, hell yea, y'all got that shit. Can't nobody see y'all."

"Y'all, what's up with that shit, fool? You are a part of this; we would not have done this shit without you."

"Quic," Lil jay turned to face him, "I told you, homie. I am through with that basketball shit."

"Yea, I know but that doesn't take from what you already did. We would not be where we are without you, Jay. You were our leading scorer. Shit, you were our best offensive player period, outside of me." Quic laughed at his own assertion.

"Outside of you," Lil Jay laughed sarcastically. "You really feeling yourself."

Quic looked at Lil Jay with a half serious look on his face, "Come on, Jay, you think you can see me?"

"Hell yea, I can see you. Cuz, don't front like we ain't went back and forth."

"What! Come on, Jay. I be tappin' that ass."

"You lucky ma shit fucked up. Otherwise, I'd take you to the court and tell you to put your money where your mouth is."

Quic laughed. He knew he had Lil Jay where he wanted him. Lil Jay had taken the bait and was on the hook; it was time to reel him in.

"Alright, badass, I got a deal for you. I gotta get ready for this playoff run, and I need to be at my best. I am gonna do some extra training. You can train with me. When you get in shape, I got five hunnit that say I not only beat you head up but that I blow you out."

The competitor in Lil Jay caused him to pause in reflection. Seconds later he spoke deliberately, "I told you I'm done with that basketball shit, Cuz."

"I know you are. It ain't gotta be about that, a head up game between homies. That's it."

"Yea, but if I go to the school to work out everybody gone be on me about playin'. Fuck all of that."

Quic smiled deviously. He wasn't letting Lil Jay off that easy, "We ain't gotta go to school. We can use the weight room here, and practice on the court in the back."

A twinkle in Lil Jays now glossed eyes answered Quic's proposition. He was in, "Ahight, Cuz, since you just wanna give a nigga yo bread, when you wanna start?"

"Today, I'll pick you up after practice."

"Bet."

Quic showed up just as he said he would. He and Lil Jay went to the weight room and engaged in a spirited upper body routine that quickly turned competitive. Lil Jay standing over six feet and weighing over 200 pounds was much stronger than the significantly smaller Quic. He didn't hesitate to let Quic know that he knew it,

"Put some mo up there, lil nigga." He instructed while lying back on the bench looking at the weight bar with four quarters on either side.

"Lil nigga, ha ha. Ahight, big guy." Quic put an additional quarter on either side," Is that it, big guy?" Quic raised his eye brows and widened his eyes in a questioning manner.

"Nah, you can put another one."

Quic did as asked. Lil Jay was unmoved. He hit the 300 pounds twice and strained out a third, an impressive feat, no doubt.

Quic knew he could not bench 300 pounds. He would not hurt himself even trying. He had Lil Jay take two quarters off each side. He then ran off a quick and comfortable ten reps. He would run the long distant marathon.

Five sets in, Lil Jay having removed several quarters was really struggling while Quic was still above seven in a set at the same weight. "You ain't burnt. Are you, big guy?" Quic teased while simultaneously motivating his boy.

"Nah, ah, ah, ahm good." Lil Jay was winded.

All in all, the fellas got a good workout in. In the end, both Quic and Lil Jay left the weight room sweaty and tight.

The work-out wasn't over. Quic guided the two-person party to the basketball court for a bit of cardio.

Though this was Quic's area and he knew he could easily upstage Lil Jay he went light. His objective was to build Lil Jay, not tear down and discourage him.

Two weeks after their first workout, Quic and Lil Jay were ready to make good on their bet. Quic wanting to complete his goal tailored the initial bet, "We are playing for $500, and I'll give you a three-point head start. If I don't win by four, I have to pay you on the spot."

"All hell yea!" Lil Jay jumped in.

"Hold on. I ain't finish. If I beat you by five, you gotta rejoin the team immediately. You gotta play in the last game plus play for the playoff run."

"Aww, Cuz, you throwin' shit in da game. I told you ahm through wit basketball."

"You plan on winnin', right?"

"Ha, ha, you funny."

"Real shit."

"Fuck it. Come on, Cuz."

Quic felt he had his boy. Despite Lil Jay's reluctance, Quic knew that Jay was a man of his word and would not back off when he lost. Quic also knew that there was no way that he would lose to Lil Jay with so much at stake.

Quic played the hardest game he'd ever played. He knew that Jay would only have a chance if he got his outside shot going, either that or if he was able to get a post-up game going. He didn't give him action at either.

Quic got in Lil Jay's face from the first. If Jay put the ball on the ground, Quic used his speed to poke it away. The ball either went out of bounds or bounced where Quic could run it down and complete the steal. In the end, Lil Jay scored only two points. Quic pretty much routed his best friend. He didn't feel bad about it either; he'd done it for a greater good.

"You lucky mothafucka. I'm still rusty," Lil Jay said in a serious yet teasing tone.

"I believe you. We'll do it like this. Keep your money. Just come back to the team. We need you, homie."

Lil Jay nodded his silent agreement, "You a slick lil bastard."

Quic laughed at what Jay thought he knew. He basked in the secret knowledge of his real objective. It was all good.

In the words of the lovely Jill Scott, "Am I my brother's keeper? Yes, I am."

Chapter Thirteen

Tighter Rope

Quic and Tasha went to the Alondra Six with Lil Jay and Kim on their 7th date as a couple. It wasn't supposed to be a double date, but Quic didn't want to let Lil Jay out of his sight for fear that he'd get caught up in something.

Quic and Lil Jay had been virtually inseparable since they'd started working out together. This kept Lil Jay out of trouble. With Quic Lil Jay never got high or drank. Quic didn't do either. Gang involvement was at a minimum. Between weight training and on court practice there wasn't much time.

Lil Jay knew what Quic was doing. He appreciated it. However, he was Park Village Crip through and through. Once out of Quic's presence Lil Jay consciously honored his hood obligations.

The beef between the Park Village Crips and Crazy Locos had intensified to a point where the Crip-Blood thing was virtually an afterthought in Park Village. Lil Jay and his Light Blue Glasshouse lived across the A line during the late-night hours. The A line was the hood term for Alondra Boulevard, the street that separated Park Village turf from that of the Crazy Locos.

Quic was none the wiser. He had no idea what Jay did after the two went their separate ways. He was naive enough to think that he was saving his friend.

The party of four was at the Alondra Six to see Eddie Murphy's star-studied "Harlem Nights," a movie that featured several top-notch comedians and promised to be hilarious. Quic and Lil Jay needed this time of relaxation to recoup after all the intense training.

Lil Jay and Kim secured the seats while Quic and Tasha went for snacks. The lines in front of the snack bars were long and crowded. Black folks were out in full force.

Quic held a spot about twelve people back with his right arm circling Tasha's waist when a familiar voice spoke from his rear, "What's up Tash?"

Tasha and Quic turned in unison. Quic's stomach dropped as Motoroil stood looking like a caricature from a horror spoof. His black-blue face looking like it had been drenched in baby oil framed pink lips and yellow teeth that needed serious dental care. His smile said that he was oblivious.

"Hi Derek," Tasha's voice was strained.

An inadvertent grimace crossed Quic's expression, and his fist clenched as he anticipated a confrontation that he truly wanted no part of.

Motoroil turned towards Quic. The smile he'd been wearing for Tasha did a summersault. "What's hattenin', dog?"

Quic chuckled, Motoroil's exaggerated mean mug and gritted teeth were comical in a way that immediately put him at ease, "What's going on, Derek?"

"What's up with your homeboy?" Motoroil smile returned.

"Which one?" Quic furrowed his eyebrows in feigned confusion.

"That little nigga, ahh."

"What's hattenin', Cuz?" Lil Jay interrupted from the rear.

Quic laughed and said, "Derek was just asking me what's up with one of my homies."

"What's up with Blood?" A short dude as dark as Motoroil backed by six or seven other high school aged individuals stepped forward.

"Fuu, ummm, wha, wha, what's up, Cuz?" Lil Jay swallowed a lump of spit.

"Fuck crab," the leader of the pack spat.

Lil Jay looked as if he was going to respond but thought better. He bowed his head slowly then in a split second lifted it back up as he threw a fast and wild over hand right. He caught his target on the temple sending him to an early nap. The other Bloods launched forward like a pack of hyenas. Quic followed suit but to no avail. The Bloods devoured Quic, Lil Jay, and even Kim, who was a Cripalet from Grape Street Watts.

Kim had hit one of the Bloods with a broom she pulled seemingly from nowhere. She got an effective hit that left the victim bloody but not out. With blood running down his face, he rushed her swinging furious fists meant for a dude. Kim crumbled to the floor and curled into the fetal position.

Tasha was smart enough not to get involved. She stood to the side and begged Motoroil and his friends to stop though her pleas fell on deaf ears. The beat down was short lived. Theater security had been on standby and responded with an impressive speediness that sent Motoroil and his homies sprinting for their freedom.

Aside from a few bumps and bruises Quic and the others were alright. They even made a bid to stay and watch the movie they'd come to see. Security wasn't having it though. They feared that Motoroil and company would return more violently.

Having come in different cars, the couples said quick goodbyes and went their separate ways. Tasha, embarrassed and afraid, wanted to be taken home. Quic, feeling horrible, obliged without protest.

Tasha wasn't mad at Quic. She was upset with herself for having been paralyzed by fear. Her conscience chided her for having not participated. A part of her feared that Quic and the others silently condemned her.

Tasha's self-accusing thoughts muted her for the entire ride home. Quic sat quietly as well. He didn't say anything because he did not know what to say. His thoughts unrelated to Tasha's were centered on how he'd fucked up and allowed himself to put Tasha's in harm's way; especially considering it was on some shit they both disagreed with.

Quic had been raised to believe that a man was supposed to be the protector of his woman, not the one who put her in harm's way.

Quic admired Kim's heart but disagreed with her actions. She should not have gotten involved. No woman should ever be beaten the way she had been. The dude who had beaten Kim up was a punk who needed to have his own ass whipped.

Quic pulled to the curb in front of Tasha's house. He put the car in neutral and continued his silence. Marvin Gaye and Tammy Terrell's "If I could Build My Whole World Around You" played low through the Mazda's stereo.

He had no idea whether he and Tasha were good or not. Tasha had told him that she was done messing with gang bangers and then his dumb ass promptly goes and gets himself caught up in a gang flight right in front of her. He was disgusted with himself.

Tasha sat in a state of confusion. Her emotions were all over the place. She was angry, embarrassed, afraid, and turned on all at the same time. Yes, turned on. Quic's display of courage despite being grossly outnumbered was so sexy to her. He held it down like a real man. The same thing that had attracted Tasha to the bad boys she had dated in the past.

Tasha had the house to herself. Her parents were at work while Indo was out doing his thing. One side of her wanted to invite Quic inside so they could have another crack at a good date, while another side of her feared that Quic's leaving the car running was a sure sign that she'd be rejected. She worried that he was angry and thought that she was a coward.

Tasha also knew that if Quic were to come inside, there was a high likelihood that their relationship would evolve to the next level. Her feelings were deep enough for Quic that if he asked her to have sex with him, she would surely say yes.

Tasha wasn't a virgin. She'd lost her virginity three years before to one of Indo's big homies. Big Black had creeped 14-year-old Tasha behind Indo's back, an easy feat for a 25-year-old with considerable experience. He simply played on Tasha's teenage insecurities. The clandestine nature of the relationship allowed him to isolate his prey, text book pedophile seduction. Tasha's saving grace came in the form of a murder robbery that left Big Black on death row. A year and a half had gone by since Big Black's incarceration separated the two. Tasha hadn't had sex since he had been arrested. She was ripe for the picking.

Quic was Tasha's guy; her homie, lover, friend. Their relationship had been a long time coming. Quic had crushed-on Tasha for years. Tasha hadn't had a crush on Quic in the same way, but she had, however, found him cute in a nerdy way. She had also found him to be cool and easy to talk to.

Things were different now. Tasha was in love with Quic. She had fallen hard. His tapered fade, Bruce Lee-like chiseled frame, and chocolate complexion were attractive to her.

"You wanna come in?" Tasha broke the silence.

"Where's your family?"

"They're not home."

Quic sat quietly; Tasha's request had caught him by surprise. The situation had gone from one extreme to another in a way that left him thoroughly confused.

"Well?" Tasha broke the silence once again.

"Yea, yea, yea, tha, tha, that's cool," his words stumbled over one another.

"I didn't ask you if it was cool. I asked if you wanted to come in. You don't have to if you don't want to."

Damn ole high strung ass sensitive girl. Quic thought. He smiled. Girls were a trip. They were cool as hell when friends but crazy as hell when girlfriends.

Quic exited his thoughts and gave Tasha the answer she was looking for, "Yea, I wanna come in."

"Okay, come on." Relief followed by a huge smile crossed Tasha's expression.

Tasha's house was plusher inside than out. The living room looked like an art exhibit. Its antique furniture, couch, love seat, and recliner chairs were all covered in plastic. There was a burnt and varnished wood grained coffee table that looked waxed. A huge picture window complimented well placed afro-centric paintings that looked expensive.

Quic didn't get to see much more as Tasha marched him through the heavily shadowed dining room and kitchen to the den. The den's shadows danced under the glow cast by the night light of a 32-gallon fish tank. Quic stood transfixed as a small Red Devil chased a young Oscar back and forth from one end of the tank to the other.

Tasha grabbed Quic's hand and guided him to an unusually long couch and motioned for him to take a seat. The task took longer than normal and left Quic sitting with his knees nearly touching his chest. The couch was abnormally low to the ground with pillows that sunk deep.

Tasha went to the kitchen and in less than a minute returned carrying two wine coolers. She wore an instantly sweet smile as she extended the black cherry flavor one to Quic. Quic didn't drink and didn't plan on starting. However, he liked where the evening was going and had no desires to derail its course. Wine coolers were taboo in the hood, a woman's drink that barely contained alcohol, one wouldn't do him any harm.

Quic downed the soda pop tasting drink in less than two minutes. When he was done, he reached forward to sit the empty bottle on the glass topped coffee table in front of him. Tasha intercepted the bottle with a swiftness that caught Quic by surprise.

"No, baby, that will leave a ring that my mom would definitely catch. Are you trying to get my ass kicked? "Tasha laughed. She grabbed both coolers by their necks and went back to the kitchen.

"Hold on." Quic shot to his feet. "Whoa," he said as he swayed and went right back down. "Shit."

He shook his head from side to side to gather himself as best he could. Realizing that he had a pretty good buzz going, he altered his approach by rising with a deliberateness that was befitting. The wine cooler had done a great deal more than he had expected.

Tasha started busting up laughing; as Quic's drunken behavior tickled her pink. She'd known that the cooler would get him drunk. Quic's being a nondrinker meant that his tolerance level was low.

"What are you laughing at?" Quic's slurred words were chased by uncontrollable laughter.

"You," Tasha said as she doubled over with laughter.

"Ha, ha, wha where y'all da damn bathroom at?"

Tasha directed Quic to the restroom without going with him. During his absence, she took the wine cooler bottles out back and stashed them deep under the trash. Her parents would kill her if they knew she and Quic had been drinking.

Back on the couch, Tasha took a seat close to Quic who had beaten her back by seconds. Quic sat stiffly and felt her warm breath on the side of his face.

Quic's experience didn't have to run deep for him to know what time it was. He turned and greeted Tasha's lips head on. He pecked her tenderly one, two, three times. He slid his tongue into her mouth and kissed her with a passion that had been pent up for far too long. Their tongues circled one another while their heads turned from side to side. Quic allowed his hands to roam Tasha's curves. Her body responded like the purring cat under the tender touch of a loving owner. Tasha's chest rose and fell rapidly as her breathing intensified.

The cooler had relieved Tasha of all inhibitions. Her hands went to work as well moving seductively up and down his spine. Quic, driven by a passion never previously tapped into, grew bold enough to remove Tasha's clothes. Her shirt was first revealing a black lace brassiere sitting on top of flawless vanilla mounds. He massaged them tenderly. His mind raced, wondering how far Tasha would let him go. *She wants' it. Why else would she let me go this far? Shit, she even got me drunk. She knows that I don't drink. She knew that shit would get me drunk*, he reasoned with himself.

Fuck it! Quic screamed inside his head before taking the plunge of lifting Tasha's brassiere above her vanilla treats. He closed his eyes and gritted his teeth bracing himself for fierce resistance.

Tasha lay back. Her young breasts topped by perky nipples that looked like the tips of removable erasers barely moved. Quic didn't need to wonder any more. He knew exactly what time it was. He leaned over her and hungrily tasted one nipple at a time. They were as sweet as advertised.

A couple minutes on the breasts and it was time to move on. Quic lifted himself back to a sitting position. He needed a visual to correctly plot his course. His eyes caught a glimpse of Tasha's red splotched vanilla thighs revealed by her elevated skirt. His hands went to work. Within seconds he'd boldly removed her black lace panties. Life moved in fast forward. Quic stood, dropped his guess jeans and light blue boxers to his knees, and mounted Tasha. He was so anxious that he did not even take a moment to eye his prize. Tasha wasn't shy or bashful; she wanted it just as bad as Quic wanted to give it to her. She grabbed Quic's maleness and guided him to her pearly gates. That was all the assistance Quic needed. He crawled into her confined space slowly the first time. It took a couple ins and outs to make a comfortable fit. With comfort achieved, Quic went to work. Five minutes later, the undisciplined lover found himself convulsing in ecstasy.

Light flooded the den, and the amplified sound of a riving engine pierced the quiet. Tasha stuck her palms in Quic's chest and pushed him off her, "Oh shit, oh, oh, oh my God. You, you, you gotta go."

"Huh, what?" Quic stood, his business dangling with semen dripping.

"That's my dad!" Tasha screamed frantically.

Quic eyes went wide with fear. He pulled his pants and boxers up nearly tripping in the process. He started for the den's exit.

"No, no, no" Tasha jumped up pulled her skirt down and adjusted her brassiere.

Quic paused and stood lost. Tasha ran to him grabbed his arms and led him to a side door off the den that led to the driveway where her dad had just parked. "Wait till you hear the front door close then leave."

"Ok," Quic said thinking *This girl is a pro. She's obviously been through this before.*

Quic followed Tasha's directions to a T and made an uncomplicated escape. He drove home listening to Marvin Gaye while sporting an ear to ear smile and feeling good.

Chapter Fourteen

Crip-Call

Lil Jay's return propelled the Tarbabe's play to another level. He led the way as the team won their last regular season game and first two playoff games in dream team fashion.

Lil Jay took Quic's place as the team's Michael Jordan averaging 35 points a game and playing shut down defense. The extra practices had built his strength and stamina, elevating him to superior athletic status.

The Tarbabes earned a spot in the state championship game and, though they entered with an 18-game winning streak, they were once again underdogs. This was justified to everyone except the

Tarbabes as their opponent, Milliken High, was undefeated on the season.

The Tarbabes knew something that no one else apparently knew; they knew their own heart, soul, hunger, and skill set. They also knew that Milliken's undefeated record had come at the hands of inferior competition. The Tarbabes knew that they were the better team and couldn't wait to prove it.

Coach White used the underdog's status to motivate his team. He had them in the film room more than normal. They watched every single one of Milliken's games for the season, studying positive and negative tendencies while looking for flaws. They broke Milliken down frame by frame.

Coach White also had his team watch film on the Detroit Pistons bad boys and the show time Lakers. He believed that great defense would win his team the championships.

The Tarbabes did not disappoint, running show time offence and shut down defense in a fashion that earned them a blowout victory. Quic, having netted 30 points, 15 assists, ten rebounds, and eight steals, was the game's unquestioned MVP. Coach White was happy for his star; however, he also wanted to reward Lil Jay whom he considered his team's unsung hero. He presented Lil Jay with the game ball and sang praises about his contributions.

The Tarbabes engaged their now ritualistic Chico's celebration once again. This time, however, they did so knowing that a much grander celebration loomed. Coach White had promised the team a trip to Hawaii contingent on them winning the championship. They couldn't wait to cash in.

After Chico's, Quic drove himself and Lil Jay back to the hood. They were surprised to see that the hood in perfect paradoxical form was a lively somber mix.

Quic intended to turn into Lil Jay's parking lot but could not. The entrance was blocked by Big He-man's El Camino parked sideways bumping Marvin Gaye through its monster sound system. He continued up the boulevard intent on settling for a spot in the next parking lot. This parking lot was blocked as well.

"Damn, Cuz," Lil Jay called out. "This mothafucka is packed. Too bad all these mothafucken niggas didn't show up to support us." He laughed before continuing. "I wonder what this is about."

Quic remained silent as he took in the scene that minus the large population presence felt eerily like the one he encountered the night Lil Jay and Black Tee had gotten shot. The memory made his stomach turn; something was wrong; he could feel it.

More people were hanging out than usual. Several mini crowds of six to seven people talked through serious and saddened expressions. Quic didn't find a spot to park until they reached the rear of the apartments near his own home. He and Lil Jay exited the car and started for the crowds of people milling about.

Red caught them before they reached the others, "What's up with y'all, Cuz?"

"Shit, just came from winning the state championship," Lil Jay smiled.

"That's right. Did y'all hear about the homie?" Red asked the duo.

"The homie?" Quic and Jay asked simultaneously.

"Yea, Cuz. Black Tee passed, Cuz. Cuz couldn't come back from that damn coma." He lowered his head and shook it slowly. Quic turned to Lil Jay whose eyes instantly became bloodshot. His first instinct was to provide a shoulder or shield to protect or keep his best friend out of the trouble the news would surely usher him into. Black Tee had been a good friend of his as well. News of his death brought a huge cloud of sadness over him, which made being happy about winning the state championship feel inherently inappropriate.

Lil Jay and Red spoke words Quic could not hear. Everything went silent for Quic. The music, the hundreds of talking people, everything, including time stopped. Quic watched from a distant place as Lil Jay and Red walked towards one of the many crowds. He waited a few seconds before spinning on his heels and going back in the direction from where he'd just come. He didn't want to be around this sadness, not at this moment, not now. He needed nonbelief, denial, he needed the protection of his mother's embrace. Reality wasn't going anywhere. It would be here awaiting his return.

Quic jumped back into the Mazda and drove out of the hood. He didn't have a conscious destination but wasn't surprised when he ended up parked in front of Tasha's house where he turned the engine and music off in favor of silence.

His thoughts guided him down a memory lane he'd had no desire to travel yet was powerless to resist.

Quic had known Black Tee for nearly as long as he had known Lil Jay. Though Black Tee was two years his senior, the two had attended all the same schools. Black Tee and Quic had bonded on the same common thread as others from Park Village had bonded on; defense from getting jumped by the Nutty Blocks at Longfellow elementary school.

Quic thought about how Black Tee's fierce loyalties coupled with a lion's heart often led to unwelcomed physical defeats. Black Tee would put in work in a New York minute but could not fight a lick. Still his worth exceeded that of most everyone around him.

Black Tee had been a family man who was an excellent provider. He had three kids by his home girl Tamika, whom he'd rented an apartment in the hood with. The thought of his kids being fatherless, the way that Quic and his little brother had been, brought tears to Quic's eyes. Quic had always said that he would not wish a fatherless childhood on his worst enemy.

A knock at his window brought Quic back to the here and now. "What are you doing?"

Tasha's lips mouthed silently. Quic lowered his window so that he could hear her. "What are you doin' out here sitting in the dark and quiet by yourself?" Tasha repeated.

Quic went to speak, but no words came out. A single tear involuntarily escaped his right eye. He placed his head in the palms of his hands. Tasha opened the car door, kneeled, and threw her arms around him; words were unnecessary.

Quic did not want to look up, he had no desire to face Tasha as his embarrassment ran too deep. Men were not supposed to cry, especially in front of their women.

Tasha didn't give that any thought. She only wanted to support her guy. She did not say a word though, choosing instead to simply hold him. She just held him. He would speak when he was ready.

Quic finally spoke after what seemed like an eternity, "You feel like taking a ride?"

Tasha didn't give it a second thought. She released Quic, closed the car door, walked around and took the passenger's seat. Her parents would be pissed, but she wasn't worried about that now.

Quic desired the quiet, soothing comfort of the highway. From Tasha's he went up Rosecrans and jumped on the 710 freeway. He took the 710 to the 91 West. "We won the state Championship." He offered out of the blue.

"I knew you guys would." Tasha smiled her beautiful smile.

Words spilled out of Quic like a broken damn. He went on and on about the game and his team, telling Tasha stuff about basketball that she didn't understand. With a smile etched across her expression, Tasha listened intently as Quic willed himself away from thoughts of Black Tee. When he finally paused his ten-minute ramble, Quic asked Tasha if she was hungry.

"Yes, kinda," Tasha was reluctant as she was still shy about letting him spend money on her.

Quic took the 110 connecting ramp with the intent to hit Rosecrans and frequent the McDonald's where he once worked.

Quic pulled into the drive-through nursing a growling stomach that had successfully kept him from thinking about Black Tee. He looked at Tasha whose beautiful face was complimented by the star-filled sky sitting beyond her shoulders. The moment transported them to a mystic reality. They were blessed, and all was well. Tasha's soft eyes were a house of love that extended Quic an invitation to enter. Neither Quic nor Tasha saw the burgundy Regal pull into the parking lot. Both were in the comfort of the world they had created together.

Quic ordered himself a McRib, fries, and coke while taking the liberty to order Tasha a fish fillet with fries and a small strawberry soda. He knew his girl that well.

The cashier's window was manned by a pretty girl with smooth skin the color of dark chocolate. She latched her brown eyes on Quic in a provocative way as she held her hand out for the payment. She obviously was oblivious to Tasha's presence. It didn't matter as Quic had not even noticed the look from the strange girl.

The pickup window was a different story. Mrs. Smith, an older sister who'd been at McDonald's for over 10 years, was there with her motherly smiled.

"Hey, Mrs. Smith," Quic forced himself to smile.

Mrs. Smith stuck her head out the window to get a closer look, "Hey, Quic. How are you, baby?"

"I'm good. How have you been?"

"I've been blessed. How's the basketball going?"

"Really good we just won the…"

"Break yourself," a thundering voice cut Quic off.

Quic and Tasha both turned in the direction of the passenger's door where the voice had come from. The sight of the cocked .38 caused Tasha to scream at the top of her lungs.

"Boom!" thundered the .38 sentencing Tasha to silence. Tasha's head snapped back then slumped forward. Quic's eyes went wide, deleting his proximity to reality leaving the screen blank. He wanted to reach forward to confront the stranger in his passenger seat. It was the appropriate thing to do if he could will the paralysis away.

The shooter paused in suspended time. His familiar eyes, warm, apologetic and afraid, peered through holes cut into the beanie covering his features. Ten seconds passed before he lowered his gun and took off running. His mind told his hands to reach forward and grab Tasha. His hands didn't listen. He tried to speak, but nothing came out.

Quic willed his right hand to the side of Tasha's bleeding face. The warm and thick wetness felt inappropriately soothing to his fingers. With an elevated heart rate and rapid breathing Quic jumped and snatched his hand back. The crimson liquid shone under the glow of the moon. A paralyzing fear penetrated his being, while his mind refused to accept what he knew had happened. The quiet still of the night was deafening.

Quic waited a long minute before putting his crimson hand back against Tasha's face. He rested here to become one with the warmth, the love of his young life's inappropriately premature departure. Involuntary tears blazed a trail down his cheeks, and his head grew heavy. What had he done? What the fuck had he done? His bullshit affiliation, yes him the non-gangbanging thug, cursed by abject poverty at the hands of an oppressive machine with genocidal tendencies. He may as well gangbang, be the Crip that people labeled him, the Crip they gave birth to and subsequently murdered in him.

Lil Jay had been shot. Black Tee had been murdered. He, Lil Jay, and Kim had been jumped. Quic's dad, rest his soul, had been killed. Tasha was gone. *Aw, fuck, Tasha, my sweet dear Tasha*, Quic sobbed loudly. It was a guttural, heart-wrenching sob. *Was he a gangster, a fucken Park Village Crip? Was he the dude draped in blue with ropes tied to his ankles and wrist? Was he too under the control of the white sheeted puppet master with the sinister grin?* This was bad, rope around the neck bad.

Quic's chest tightened, the strength left his body, and he felt nauseous. "I'm sorry. I am so sorry, Tasha. I never meant for this to happen. I swear to God. God is my witness."

"Quic, Quic," a soft voice whispered. Reality pointed him in the direction of the voice prompting him to sit up and focus. Was Tasha calling him? Had she survived? Had the blood been the product of a paranoid hallucination? "Quic, are you guys okay?" It wasn't Tasha.

Quic turned to look over his left shoulder and found a terrified Mrs. Smith. "No, no, no ca, ca call the an ah um amb amb bu la lance, pa please." Quic's tears were in free fall, and he did not try to hide them.

After two minutes that felt more like an hour passed by Quic heard another voice. "What the fuck?" The disrespectful mouth called out in an exaggerated manner.

Quic did not look up, nor did he respond. He heard them, the no-good entity that was nothing short of terror on the hood, the legal Crips and Bloods, the big bad wolf, yes, them. He did not want to talk though.

"What's up, Cuz? What happened here? Busta ass slobs caught y'all slippin'?" The words were spoken in an exaggerated slang, some shit from a television movie, some shit that only racist police would say.

Quic looked up. He had to as his stomach turned threatening to release its thin contents. His eyes crashed into the view of the blond-haired, freckled-face police officer known to Compton residents as Opie. *This racist mothafucka. Why couldn't it be somebody like his dog ass getting smoked? The world would not miss him. Even his rancid ass wife and Nazi ass kids would not miss him.*

"Who was it, Cuz? Did you see their face? Give me a description. How many were there? What's your name? Where you from? Who you run with?"

"What?" Anger steeled Quic's nerves, "What the fuck you talkin' about? Where the fuck is the ambulance?"

"They are on their way. We need to know though. Who are you? What is your name? Who is she? Is she your friend? Where are you guys from? What kind of gun were you shot with? Wamp, wamp, wamp." The cop changed tactics and began speaking proper English.

Quic was furious. He wished that he had a gun and immunity. He would take the pigs head off.

Quic was pulled from the car, searched and seated on the curb that snaked around the drive thru, he said nothing further. He endured the criminal treatment in a disengaged fog. Quic did not have an intellectual comprehension of the black man's struggle in America, the systemic oppression, the genocidal history. However, like the winos loitering in the liquor store parking lots, he knew that black folk were up against it in what he knew to be a white man's world.

From the curb, Quic was handcuff and placed in the back seat of an unmarked police car. Here, his mind drifted to a long-forgotten past.

Quic was five years old. He his mom and dad lived in a duplex not far from the Wilmington Arms. The Compton police had been called to break up a disturbance where a young adult had gotten caught trying to steal a hard-working neighbor's car. The neighbor who had caught him gave him a thorough beat down, one sanctioned by the residential collective many of whom had at some point had their own car stolen.

The Compton police saw things different. They went at the hard-working neighbor aggressively talking mess and ultimately placing him in handcuffs.

Quic's dad had been livid. "Let him go, you dumb ass racist mothafuckas. Let both of them go. The mothafuckin Panther's had it right. We need to police our own mothafuckin communities."

Quic was too young to fully comprehend what was going on. He agreed with his dad who was his hero, but he had no idea what was being said or done. This wasn't the case now. Sitting in the back of the police car nursing a shattered heart he had a hatred for the police that words could not expres

Chapter Fifteen

Nightmare

Quic stumbled backwards tripping over his own feet as the limping silhouette advanced through the shadows. The oversized couch prevented him from falling. He grabbed the couches arm to steady himself while keeping his bugged eyes on the shadowed presence.

Once he was steadied on his feet, Quic placed his outstretched arms hands open in front of him to halt the advance, "Who is that?" His voice was constricted.

The silhouette continued its advance without responding. Quic gripped by a rising terror allowed his intimate knowledge of his home's interior to guide a retreat that was on the verge of becoming hasty. He snaked his way around the couch before reverse moon walking to the apartments front door. Just as he dropped his right arm and reached behind for the door knob, an angelic voice called out, "Michael."

Quic froze; his jaw dropped and his breathing became a heavy hiss looped in reverb.

The silhouette continued forward stepping from the shadows into Quic's view. She had silky skin the color of vanilla cream and green eyes that glowed under a fogged vision. She was heavenly in an appearance that had been sculpted by the hands of God. Tasha stopped in front of Quic standing at an angle that allowed him a view of her left profile. Quic released the doorknob and put his arm and hand back in front of himself, his fearful halt became an unfulfilled desire for the beautiful queen that had been taken from him. Tasha had returned. God really did answer prayers.

Tasha flashed her million-dollar smile, the smile she'd smiled only minutes before she'd been taken. Quic reached forward to touch Tasha's cheek to make sure that she was real, that the person in front of him was really her. Her skin was soft like butter and tender to the touch. It was her. It was really her.

Tasha's smile dropped, giving way to a tear-jerking explosion. Her eyes clouded before turning bloodshot leaving Quic perplexed. He reached for her silky tenderness the butter melted and was now boiling hot. "Ouch, shit," Quic said before snatching his hand back. Liquid dripped from Quic's finger tips, "What the fuck!" Tasha's skin was melting.

Tasha turned to face Quic full on displaying a haunting smile that topped rotten teeth. Quic screamed, but nothing came out. Tasha reached forward and grabbed him by the throat crushing his windpipe and obstructing his breathing.

"Kiss me, baby," Tasha's voice was raspy like a seasoned chain smoker.

Quic looked from the melted beauty side of Tasha's face to the other and nearly collapsed at the sight of a bullet hole surrounded by dried blood sitting just above her disfigured eye. There was no denying the fact that the girl standing in front of Quic was Tasha. Quic's eyes glossed over as his mind had been completely blown. He had gone mad; of this he was sure. There was no other explanation. He ordered his arm to knock Tasha's hand away; nothing. Tears left his eyes as he felt consciousness leaving him.

"Do you still love me, baby? Do you? Answer me, Michael."

"Michael, Michael, Michael," another voice called from a distant place.

Quic's eye's shot open, and though groggy he could breathe. Tasha's horrific image was replaced by the confronting beauty of his caramel complexioned mother.

"Are you okay baby?" Mrs. Green's expression was that of a concerned mother. "Ye, ye, yea, ma, ah ah ahm okay." Quic ran his open palm across his sweat drenched face.

"You sure, baby? You were screaming in your sleep."

"Are you sure, ma? Ah, I wasn't even dreaming about anything."

Mrs. Green knew that her son's pride had him lying, yet she would let it go. He would talk to her when he was ready. "Ok, baby, Jeffrey is on the phone. Do you want to talk to him?"

"Yes, ma. I'll talk to him. Let me get up."

Quic got up from his twin bed and grabbed the telephone from his dresser while shaking the cobwebs. "What's going on, Jay?" he wanted to put the dream as far behind him as possible.

"Cuz, I need you." Lil Jay's words were properly pronounced and deliberate.

"What's up?" Quic sighed sensing some gang bull involvement that he had no stomach to deal with.

"Can't say any particulars but I'm in Tree Top over Sunny's house, and I need a ride."

"I don't have my car. They took it."

"Damn, no shit, I forgot. Fuck it. Go get mines. I'll have my mother give you the keys."

"You not in your car?"

"Nah, I'll explain when you come."

Quic did as Lil Jay had requested and within minutes was on the road looking like the gang banger that he wasn't. He could only hope that the Tree Tops did not mistake him for a Crip and shoot the car up.

Lil Jay sat on Sunny's porch sporting black khakis and a blue Pendleton like he didn't have a care in the world; as if the Pirus over there wouldn't tear his head off if given a chance. Quic shook his head at the absurdity.

"Yaah!" Jay leaped to his feet.

"Get yo ass in," Quic was upset.

"Damn grouchy, Cuz," Lil Jay slammed the door behind him.

"It ain't like that, homie."

"Whatever. Peep, Cuz, guess what?"

"What's going on?"

"I got that bitch ass nigga."

"Who?"

"That busta ass fool Motoroil. On PV, I knocked his bitch ass down. Fo you, fo me, fo Black Tee, fo you girl, fo Crip!"

Motoroil, the Piru that Lil Jay knew, symbolized Piru and everything Pirus had done in opposition to the Crip that Lil Jay represented. Lil Jay having apparently murdered him was overwhelmingly yet unnaturally happy. His eyes were wild with excitement.

"Quic, I caught that fool on the corner in his hood with several of his homies, I aired their ass out, on Harry-o Cuz."

Quic listened intently not sure how he should feel about what he had heard. He hadn't known exactly who murdered Tasha nor had he known which Piru pulled the trigger on the gun that took Black Tee's life. Yet, like Lil Jay, he believed that Motoroil represented all that was in opposition not only to Crip but himself as well.

"How did you get over Sunny's house?" Quic finally asked.

"One time got on us after we dumped those fools out. F-dog hit slobcrans on two wheels in the g-ride we had snatched from down town. I did some TV shit. I opened my door and hit the pavement rolling. Car chases always go bad if you don't get out the car before the bird hits the air. I ain't goin' down fo no hot one, fuck that. I jumped up bent the corner, tucked the strap in some bushes and ran to Sunny's."

"Damn,"

"Did F-dog make it back?" Lil Jay wanted to know.

"I don't know. I'd been in the house all night."

Quic was talking to Lil Jay, but he really wasn't present. Tasha was dead. Black Tee was dead. Motoroil was dead. And Lil jay had found himself on both ends of the gun. Shit was crazy.

The Wilmington Arms was dry when Quic and Lil Jay returned. It was like a real-life ghost town, a regular day that in no way was a normal day. Quic parked in the front near Lil Jay's house, gave Jay his keys, and walked home. Quic was half way up the boulevard when the ghost town came to life with several cries of "One time." The cries were followed by thunderous footsteps. Homies and friends appeared from the shadows trying to get out of dodge. *They may as well have stayed where they were.* Quic thought as he continued walking.

"It's a raid," an unidentifiable voice stated the obvious from a distance as patrol car after patrol car sped through the gate making sharp left turns into the parking lot that Quic had just left.

A 10-patrol car presence in the Wilmington Arms wasn't out of the usual. Still, it was clear that this wasn't a typical raid. Compton police were on a mission that was tailored and targeted. Quic's stomach turned as their intended destination dawned on him.

"Fuck," Quic spent on his pivot. "Lil Jay," he called running back towards where he'd left his best friend.

Quic bent the corner in time to see Lil Jay being pushed in the back seat of a patrol car driven by the Compton police everyone knew as Blondie.

Lil Jay's sad expression broke Quic's heart, as he knew what Lil Jay's charge would be. Quic once again pivoted and went in the opposite direction. It was time to go home and pray that he did not get railroaded into some type of erroneous involvement.

Lil Jay's mother told Quic later that the police said her son was being charged with one murder and four attempted murders. He would be arraigned within 72 hours and that no one would have any contact with him for one week at minimum. They explained to her that juveniles were placed in isolation for this period upon being charged with murder. This was customary in California.

The detectives also told Lil Jay's mother that F-dog had been arrested and he too had been taken to juvenile hall and charged with one murder and four attempted murders.

Quic's head was a sea of confusion for the next couple weeks. It didn't help that Big Indo and the rest of his Mob homies hit him with several accusingly evil eyes throughout Tasha's funeral. They obviously blamed him for Tasha's murder.

Quic's confusion deepened when he learned that Motoroil had not been murdered and, in fact, was the witness who'd identified Lil Jay and F-dog. Lil Jay had told his mom to tell Quic that Motoroil had told the police that he and his friends had been targeted by Lil Jay and F-dog because the two thought that they had murdered Black Tee and Tasha. Motoroil was the sole person to identify Lil Jay and F-dog. Quic was hood conscious enough to comprehend the message that Lil Jay was indirectly sending. Motoroil needed to come up missing for Lil Jay and F-dog to have a chance at coming home.

Quic didn't gangbang, but Lil Jay was his best friend. The weight of the situation took up residences on Quic's shoulders causing his back to stoop.

Chapter Sixteen

Cross-Roads

It was two days before Lil Jay's second court appearance. The appearance where the prosecutions sole witness was due to take the stand. The appearance that would determine whether Lil Jay and F-dog would be imprisoned for the remainder of their young lives.

Quic was the only person in the neighborhood who knew who Motoroil was. This gave him proximity. For this reason, the non-gang banging kid with unlimited potential was being promoted to the majors.

Ready or not Quic's first at bat was approaching. The stress on his face like an uncomplicated novel was easy to read. He'd had fist fights in defense of his best friend and what he represented.

However, Quic had never sustained any serious injuries, nor had he seriously injured anyone. Picking up a gun and shooting someone was a bird of a completely different feather. This was foreign terrain for the kid.

Quic was wandering around the Wilmington Arms early Saturday morning. Overwhelmed by the daunting task, he decided to seek guidance.

Quic found Red sitting on the steps leading to the second tiered apartment in G building. "What's going on, homie?" Quic extended his hand.

"What's up with you?" Red shook Quic's hand.

"Can I pop at you real quick?" Though Quic wasn't a vet, he knew that inviting too many people into his confidence was not a good idea. The more people knew what was going on, the higher the possibility of getting caught.

Red dismounted the stairs adjusting his sagging sweats, "Let's walk."

With Red leading the way the two started for the rear of the apartment complex, "What's on your mind, Cuzin?" Red said tugging at his Dodger's baseball cap.

"Lil Jay told me who was snitching on him." Quic ran his open hand down his face.

"I know. I heard it's some slob nigga you play basketball with."

Quic gave Red a sideways glance that questioned the fact that he was already aware of who was snitching and yet hadn't done anything.

"Jay said that dude is the only evidence against him."

"Is that right?"

"Yea, Lil Jay said if dude don't show up, they gotta let him and F-dog go." Red could not miss the message, however, to be sure Quic continued, "Jay asked me to handle it."

Red smiled. He, like everyone else in the hood, knew that Quic was not a banger. This had to be a messed-up situation for him. Red empathized.

Quic wasn't exactly jumping into gang banging at this moment. Motoroil dying had no meaning to him other than the fact that he represented Lil Jay and F-dog's freedom in addition to retribution for the entity behind Tasha's and Black Tee's deaths. Truth be told, he wished his nemesis dead but didn't know how he felt about being the one that took his life.

Red still smiling said, "I got you, Cuz. When does the homie go back to court?"

"Monday."

"Damn, you know where fool at?"

"Yea, Tasha had shown me where he lived before she passed."

A dark cloud shadowed Quic's face at the mentioned of Tasha.

"Ahight, we on it today. I gotta send D-mo to get a gee." Red said referring to the older homie who though a down and out drug head was a professional car thief.

"So, we gonna meet here later?" Quic asked Red.

"Yea, at like six."

Quic and Red went their separate ways. Red went back to hustling while Quic went home and rested in his thoughts. Quic was conscious of the crossroads that his mere existence rested in at this moment. He was the duality that constituted African-American culture, the duality spoke on by Richard Wright, Ralph Ellison, and so many others.

Quic thought about how much he hated Motoroil as memories of Motoroil's misdeeds played on a loop. Motoroil had sucker punched Quic, he'd been responsible for the Incident at the Alondra Six, Motoroil's complicity in Black Tee's murder, the taunting, the beating of Tasha, and Tasha's murder, right or wrong Quic put Motoroil's face behind the mask the assailant wore,

Quic squeezed his eyes tightly shut. Tears streaked his cheeks, but he wasn't crying. This is what he told himself repeatedly.

Quic was conscious of the fact that success was not a certain. There was a possibility that he and Red would get caught and end up right alongside Lil Jay and F-dog in Los Padrinos. Everything he'd worked on to this point to get himself out of the hood would be in jeopardy. No pro basketball, no Michael Jordan dreams. Nothing.

A migraine pulsed in Quic's head, "Boomp, boomp, boomp." He tried to will it away, but it rebelled.

At 3:00 that evening Quic exited his thoughts and started getting ready. He geared himself in black Dickies, a black T-shirt, black on black Nikes, and topped it off with a Raiders baseball cap. Coming "Straight Outta Compton" Quic was Eazy E minus the Jerry curl.

At 3:20 Quic excited the house and headed to the hood's basketball court. He had two hours and forty minutes to waste.

There was a fierce battle being waged between hood stars who, though skilled, had missed their opportunities to do something with their talents. Quic sat on the sideline and wondered if this would be his lot.

If things did not go right, Quic would be another brother added to the lengthy list of hood Pee Wee Kirkland's. Quic thought about this along with several other things as his noisy mind set ablaze by uncontrollable nerves ran wild.

Anxious anticipation got the better of Quic. He started pacing the sideline like a coach with a National championship on the line. A peek at his $19.00 Timex every couple minutes informed Quic that time was crawling by.

After an hour passed Quic jogged over to the rendezvous spot, he couldn't wait anymore. This did nothing to calm his anxious impatience. He turned the carport entrance into his basketball court sideline, once again pacing to and fro. This lasted 30 to 45 minutes until his legs tired. He then took a seat against the dented trunk of a broken-down Buick.

Red showed up at five minutes after five. T-loc swooped up in his mom's Nissan Maxima. This was plan B as D-Mo had not been able to steal a car on such short notice. In short order, the trio was on the road.

From the Wilmington Arms, they went to Cedar Block on the street of the address that Tasha had given Quic for Motoroil. They found Christmas in the form of Motoroil shooting dice while surrounded by fifteen of his homies. Red instructed T-loc to park around the corner and leave the car on while he and Quic walked to the crowd and handle their business.

The time of reckoning had come. It was time for Quic to shit or get off the pot. Quic's thoughts went to *"Boyz in the Hood." Trey's eyes grew sad and even fearful.* Quic and Red had now exited the car and were pushing towards the corner's turning point in slow motion. *Trey looked ahead his eyes glossed with tears that were ready to fall.* Quic's gun was tucked under his T-shirt not easily viewable. He and Red rounded the corner. The Pirus deep into their dice game did not notice them right away.

Quic and Red walked past one house, two houses, three houses and were less than thirty feet away. *The tears escaped Trey's eyes.*

"Let me out." He sent the words in the air. He looked around one more time. "Doh, let me out."

The Pirus stood and looked in Quic and Red's direction, and all started backing away. Quic was baffled. How had they noticed them suddenly? He looked to Red. Red wore a menacing grimace on top of skin that had literally turned Red. His fist was wrapped tightly around the butt of his Glock. Quic now had the answer to his question. In a moment, he transformed into dirty Hairy. Without a second thought, he cursed Trey.

"Fuckin' punk bitch," he wasn't himself anymore. The 44 gave a kick that caused his arm to jerk.

"Shit!" Quic liked it. It was orgasmic. "Bl-owl, bl-owl, bl-owl, bl-owl," *My God* Quic thought as the Pirus scattered screaming and hollering. This was point-guard duties in the state championship game. Nah, this was more. Quic was a star. No, he was more. Dare he say it, Quic at this moment, wielding so much power, the power over life and death, was, shit, shit, shit, he was God. He was fucking GOD. GOD DAMN YOU. HE WAS GOD.

"Quic, Quic, Cuz, come on." Red tugged at the sleeve of Quic's shirt.

"Huh, what?" Quic snapped from his daze as he could hear the continuous click of his own gun. Quic released the trigger. He came completely back to the moment.

"Come on, fool, fo you get us killed." Red tugged at Quic's sleeve again.

Quic gave in and together he and Red took off full speed to the getaway car. T-loc was on point. They made a clean get away.

Quic found himself in an emotional vortex during the ride back to the Wilmington Arms. T-loc had turned the music off, and no one uttered a word. The car's interior possessed the quiet of a sanctuary.

Terror came over Quic. What had he done? Who had he become? Had he committed murder? "Oh shit, oh my God, God, please forgive me, please, please, please." Quic closed his eyes and quietly began lord prayers," Our father, who art in heaven, hallowed be thy name. Thy kingdom come, Thy will be done on earth as it is in heaven. Give us this day our daily bread and forgive us for our sins as we forgive others. And lead us not in to temptation but deliver us from evil. For thine is the kingdom and the power and glory. Amen.

<u>ABOUT THE AUTHOR</u>

Laurence Perry is a self-taught writer who in the spirit of Richard Wright, Ralph Ellison, Alice Walker, Toni Morrison, and The Harlem Renaissance Era desires to protest, educate, an uplift through true and responsible literary depiction. Pivotal Paths is his first effort. Stay tuned.